Christmas 2009 was one of the worst times in Tamzin's life as she was torn away from her delightful future with her boy-friend, Dequan, by her parents' machinations. Living unhappily under a new identity, Tamzin ran away to fairy land—literally.

Ten years passed and Tamzin was back in New South Wales. Christmas 2018 was unfulfilling, spent with her friends Gillan and Branok St Ives when she longed to be with her new love, Matin.

Christmas 2019 brings its own challenges, but at last Tamzin is exactly where she wants to be. Life is good, personally, professionally and socially. Life would be almost perfect if it weren't for the lingering shadows of her past.

Tamzin is living quite close to where she was in 2009, but it isn't the city of Sydney that holds the answers she feels on the tip of her tongue. A birthday trip to a gallery opening in Adelaide seems an unlikely catalyst, but it's there at Gallery Spenser that Tamzin faces her memories head on. Finally she learns the truth about the identity switches of her early years, but the question remains—why? Only three people know the answer, but will they be willing to talk?

Being Tamzin 6
Copyright © 2022 Lark Westerly
ISBN: 978-1-4874-3428-1
Cover art by Martine Jardin

Published by eXtasy Books Inc

Look for us online at:
www.eXtasybooks.com

BEING TAMZIN 6

BY

LARK WESTERLY

Dedication

For Tina, Jay, Cat and Bri . . . the mighty women who helped me to bring Being Tamzin to life

AUTHOR'S NOTE

The *Fairy in the Bed* series features a sprawling cast of characters who wander in and out of one another's stories. For more about this series, visit Lark's website at https://larksinger.weebly.com

The seven volumes of *Being Tamzin* tell Tamzin's story, but some of the other characters will be familiar via the following books.

Dequan Qin first appeared in *Queen of the May,* and his romance is told in *Geese a Laying,* and *Just Eloped.*

Lucy Tan first appeared in *The Pear Tree.* She fell in love with Paris in *Queen of the May.*

Nelis Winter and Xavier Partridge got together in *The Pear Tree,* which is also where Nelis met Frances and Niall. Their continuing story is told in *Being Tamzin 1* and *Being Tamzin 7.*

Flick Dark has appeared in a number of books. She met her husband in *Tied up in Tinsel.*

Tamzin appeared in a tiny part in the *Counterpoint* books and then again in the *Queen of Tarts* trilogy.

Otto, who assisted in Rochelle's escape, met Nelis in *The Pear Tree,* and encountered Lucy and Dequan in *Queen of the May.*

Pen Inkersoll first appeared in *Pen and Ink,* and Dan Fanshaw is from the *Counterpoint* series. Magda Quest is from the *Pixie Grip* series.

Like *Queen of the May, Being Tamzin* is partly set in 2020 and 2021. When I wrote *QotM,* Covid19 wasn't even thought of. By the time it was published, we were in the middle of a pandemic. Since it was far too late to rewrite the story, I had to let it be. That decision in turn affected all the other books in this timeline. My philosophy is that as the world of *Fairy in the Bed* is not *quite* our world, we can accept that in that reality the pandemic didn't happen in 2020.

Timeline:

Being Tamzin 1- 2009-2013

The Pear Tree—2011 and 2019 Nelis and Xavier—Begins during Being Tamzin 1 and ends at the beginning of Being Tamzin 6

Queen of the May—2011- 2020 Lucy and Paris Begins during Being Tamzin 1 and continues during Being Tamzin 7
Being Tamzin 2—2013—2017
Being Tamzin 3—July 2017—late November 2018
Being Tamzin 4—Late November 2018—March 2nd, 2019
Being Tamzin 5-July 2019—December 2019
Being Tamzin 6—December 2019—March 2020
Being Tamzin 7-March 2020- April 2021

Geese a Laying—2020 Dequan and Martina during Being Tamzin 7

Just Eloped—December 2020 Martina's nieces, Chiara and Lili, and Yannick—during Being Tamzin 7
Queen of Tarts trilogy—2020-late 2021, finishing after Being Tamzin 7

CHAPTER ONE: AFTER THE HOT

Tamzin Herrick, Delphinium Island, Christmas Morning 2019

Tamzin lay in a bed stuffed with springyweed and the rustling dry seaweed known as seadown. She was exhausted, with a deep weariness that came from no more than two hours of intermittent sleep, a great deal of exercise, and considerable emotional investment. She raised her arms above her head and watched the light from the rising sun gild her skin and flash shards of colour from the betrothal ring she wore on her right hand.

"Tea, mistress?"

"Yes please!" Too tired to support the strain, she let her arms flop to her sides.

She felt the bed rock slightly as Matin got in beside her.

"Do you need to go again?" she asked.

For answer, he took her hand in both of his and brought it down to his groin.

She palpated the warm, heavy mass between his thighs and sighed. "That's a no, then."

"Definitely a no," Matin said.

Tamzin closed her fingers in a caressing movement and pouted. "Does that mean I don't get a Christmas rogering?"

"Do you want one? I doubt if I can rise to the occasion, yet, but I can always help you out somehow." He made a move to sit up.

"No, thank you," she said, laughing. "I've been helped comprehensively for hours on end. I hope we didn't scare the

1

gulls."

"So do I." He settled again, stroking her hand where she still held him. "Are you . . ." He trailed off, and she heard him swallow.

"I'm perfectly all right. Just tired."

"I'm not surprised."

"I expect you are too," she said fairly. "It was you who had to keep powering on. I could have chosen to just lie there and work out logic puzzles."

"You didn't, though."

She tickled his balls. "Where's the fun in that?"

"Fun," he said, as if it was an odd concept.

"Well, I hope it was more fun for you than last year. It was certainly better for me. Last year, I was trying to hold an intelligent conversation with Bran and Gill and all the time picturing you pleasuring elf maids at the orgy. I was *so* envious — or do I mean jealous — I could barely function."

"While *I* was trying to pleasure myself and failing."

She moved one hand provocatively, stroking and pulling gently. "Is that a twitch I feel, Master Campania?"

"No."

"It is! It's a twitch. He's doing his best to stand to attention."

"I thought you were tired."

"I'm so tired I can't think straight. And my throat has a tickle." She coughed.

"That's from all the squealing you were doing in the night. Drink your tea."

"I remember you roaring a fair bit too."

"Probably when you tried to swallow my cock while wringing my balls like a teabag."

"Did I?"

"Well . . . I certainly hope it was you."

She got up on one elbow and picked up the teacup he had

set on the wooden sea chest beside the bed. She drank the tea thirstily, then she set it aside and curled down against him.

"Do you want breakfast?" he asked.

"Not yet. I just want to snuggle with you."

If he made any answer, Tamzin didn't hear it. She was asleep.

When she woke again, the sun was slanting through at a different angle, and she was hungry. She sat up, pushing her hair away from her face.

Matin stood at the window, looking out across the water. He had dressed in a hip-length tunic, three-quarter pants and soft shoes, standard wear for fay men who weren't somewhere they needed to *pass* as human.

"Hmm?" She made a questioning sound and noticed with pleasure that a fresh mug of tea and a plate of bread and honey awaited her attentions.

Her betrothed turned to smile at her. "I thought we might have a look around the island, if you feel up to it."

"I will once I get this down me." She still felt wrung out, but she was determined not to show any weakness. If Matin had spent the night with an elf maid instead of the all-too-human Tamzin, they would probably be out rock-hopping already.

"Has the Hot really gone off now?" she asked.

He hesitated. "It's not just like snapping a switch, but it's down to a gentle simmer. This was the nicest one I ever spent."

"Ooh. Really?"

"Really. Last year was by far the worst, but mostly it's a case of debriefing various partners and making awkward farewells, before going away alone and trying to make sense of it all."

"I wonder how Olivier managed," she said.

"What?" Matin sounded startled.

"Well, he's—what, twenty? And Nessa said she wasn't going to bed him for a while, if ever. He's so fond of her, though, so how would he feel about bedding someone else, or lots of someones, when he was just longing to be with her?"

"I don't know. That's his business."

"He couldn't exactly tell her how much he wanted her, either, because that would look like blackmail. Maybe he took care of it himself."

"After my experience last year, I wouldn't wish that on anyone, let alone my little brother."

She shied away from the painful thought, but she couldn't quite leave it alone. "Matin, *why* do elves get the Hot?"

"I don't think anyone has ever figured that out, for sure."

"If you could do something—take something—to avoid it, would you?"

He seemed to consider that. Then he said, "No. I can't speak for others, but I wouldn't. It's a part of who and what I am. And when it's working the way it should, with a willing lover who is there for me today and forever, then it's marvellous."

"Even when you're roaring."

He gave her a quick grin. "Especially then. It's pure release. I feel like a shooting star."

Tamzin sighed and decided to change the subject. "I wonder how Fou is."

"Being overindulged with pisky delicacies, I expect," Matin said, flipping from the intensely personal to the objective without a blink.

Tamzin considered her temporary dog, the Pekingese Fou, whom she was minding until his owners returned from wherever they had gone. *Interstate,* Breezy Barrett had said, but she hadn't said where, or why, or for how long. And her partner, Clem, hadn't said anything at all. Clem seemed pretty laidback, or maybe pretty subservient. Tamzin hadn't worked out which. Her Rembrandt-styled hat suggested someone with more to her than her habitual reticence proclaimed.

A middle-aged peke with a flowing brindled coat wasn't the type of dog Tamzin had ever envisaged when she pictured herself with a canine companion, but she was in no hurry to return him. His accepting personality had been a calm influence while she anticipated spending Matin's Hot with him. She'd pretended to be confident, but inside, she'd been increasingly nervous. What if she couldn't handle it after all? She would never desert him, but Matin would know if she felt overwhelmed and he'd try to hold back for her sake.

But that hadn't happened. It had been intense, and she was tired, but after all, she loved sex with her betrothed and routinely went for round two, so what was a few more? It was only once a year.

Fou was staying with her friends Gillan and Branok while she and Matin were on the island. Branok was Tamzin's solicitor and advisor, and he and Gill were the nearest things she had to functional parents since parting from her own in 2010.

She finished her breakfast and got out of bed. "Do I smell orange juice? Or—" She broke off, bending to pick up the underwear she'd shed the night before.

She pulled it on, then got back on the bed to kneel in a consciously provocative pose. "Ooh, I'm framed!"

She gestured to the window that looked out on a natural screen of plants, some of which had encroached on the veranda that formed the outer wall of the room.

"Very artistic," Matin said dryly. He handed her a glass of fruit juice. "It's not orange. It's—"

Tamzin sipped it and gave him a delighted grin. "Whatever it is, there's *want you so* juice in this! You cheeky thing!"

"Most of it's apple and passionfruit," he said defensively.

"Passionfruit!"

"I thought you'd like it."

"I do!" She drank it down and held out the glass for him to take. She held the pose. "Dress me?"

"What an idle maid you are." Matin clicked his fingers, and Tamzin got off the bed and smoothed down the green dress that had appeared on her body. It was the one she'd bought when she was seventeen to wear when she attended her Year Twelve formal with her first boyfriend, Dequan. Miraculously, it still fitted, and despite so many years of adventuring, it still looked new.

Her feet were encased in stylish shoes with multi-coloured heels. They were the most comfortable pair she had ever owned, and they had once belonged to Matin's sister, Misty.

"Thanks," she said. "Matin?"

"Beloved?" He stood smiling down at her, smelling oddly but delightfully of fresh green peas.

"What made you pick *these* clothes?"

"What's wrong with them?"

"Nothing. I just wondered how you chose."

"I didn't. These are just what came when I conjured *dress Tamzin.*"

Tamzin gave up. In the eighteen months she had been Matin's lover, he had never, aside from one expressed desire to have her in her ballgown, made a comment about her clothes or the way she wore her hair. But then—

"I like your tunic. Is it new?"

"Not very, but you probably haven't seen it before. It's the one I generally wear at Christmas. Hence the cherries." He touched the fine band of embroidery that lapped his collar and ran down the neckline of the tunic. "Misty has a gown with purple grapes on it, and Olivier's Christmas tunic has strawberries. It's a kind of family tradition."

"Would it be appropriate if I joined in with it once we're married?"

"I hope you will! Lars did."

"Oh?" Tamzin contemplated the vision of Misty's huge husband decorated with fruit embroidery. "What does he have—apples? Watermelons?"

"No, he has ears of wheat."

"Ah. I think *I'll* have apples."

"I'm sure you'll look delicious." He held out his hand and led her outside.

CHAPTER TWO: THE ISLAND

Tamzin Herrick, Delphinium Island, Christmas Morning 2019

Tamzin looked behind to appreciate the unusual design of Delphinium House. It had been built when a ship ran aground on the island back in the early nineteenth century, and Tamzin wondered if it incorporated some of the timbers from the ship. She remembered vaguely having heard of the *Delphinium* story, but Matin had given her few details when he'd suggested it as a good place to spend Christmas Eve.

"I wonder why the owner doesn't live here," she said. There was no electricity, but the owner was a fairy, so that would hardly be a problem.

"It's a bit of a rigmarole. Master St Ives knows the ins and outs of it."

The grounds around the house bore a surprisingly colourful garden, with self-seeding annuals, rioting succulents, and a grove of raspberry canes hung with fruit. Tamzin pointed to some sacking bundles from which branches protruded. "It's the wrong time of year to plant fruit trees."

"Is there a wrong time?"

"Isn't there? Aren't they usually put in in winter?"

"I expect so." He sounded absent, and she tugged at his hand, looking at him suspiciously.

"Master Campania, what are you up to?"

"I thought we might plant these while we're here."

Tamzin wondered if they'd planted something already. Matin always took care of contraception, since he could do it by some concentration of will unavailable to humans. Her halfling friend, Dahlia "Daylight" Pengellis, had warned her his concentration might fail during the Hot. Matin had agreed it was possible, but Tamzin had elected not to adopt human-style contraception.

If a baby happened, then it would happen. They would welcome it and love it as much as Matin's sister loved her little son, Dickon.

Tamzin had borrowed Dickon now and again, and, as with Fou, she was never in a hurry to give him back. As for Matin, like most elves he loved children, and seeing him caring for Dickon always made Tamzin's heart melt.

If it happens, we'll choose a lovely name and answer questions and we won't treat him, or her, like an appendage to be dragged about the countryside and kept in the dark.

A familiar bitterness rose in her, and she jammed it aside. She hadn't seen her parents for years—not since an unhappy young elf man had helped her to escape a confusing and miserable life as Rochelle Marlowe. She was going to find Ada and Mister Sinister, though. For months, she'd been patiently seeking clues and pursuing hints and distant memories.

Nanny Lu — Lucida.

Fiddle music. Falling.

My name was Zandie, then.

Matin squeezed her hand. "Come back, Tamzin."

"Was I drifting again?"

"A bit."

"Zen held my hand so I wouldn't drift when he used *influence* to help me remember Zandie," she said.

"I should hope so!"

"And he wiped my face for me when I cried, and he gave me a cup of tea."

"I see."

"He said he'd get me a coffee from the *Paws a While* van. He went off, and I think he met up with Dahlia and forgot about me."

"And the coffee came, but Zen came not," Matin intoned. "Did he happen to answer your thank-you text at all?"

"Eventually, but he didn't *say* anything. He's exasperating."

"Young brothers always are."

Tamzin smiled. "It's nice having them, though, even if they're foster brothers like Zennor and Mull. Did I ever tell you Zen offered to have Demi-dog bite you if you forgot to appreciate me?"

"You did not."

"I told him it wouldn't be necessary."

Matin stopped her with a tug. "Never mind about your foster-brothers. I'm glad you have them, and that they care for you as brothers should, but what do you think of the island?"

She breathed in the scent of salt and flowers. "Umm, smells delicious. You'd never think we were so close to a major city. You've been here before, so show me around."

He said, "You like the sea air, I expect?"

"Very much. That's one of the reasons I love living at Fiddler's Rest. It reminds me of my time with the fleet."

"You must have enjoyed that, since you spent so long sailing with the galleonfee."

"Yes. Three or so years, depending on whether I count time ashore. One of my favourite things was standing near the figurehead and looking out to sea. I miss that — and I even miss Stella Orris. Did I ever tell you about that?"

"Not in any detail."

"Maybe it was Bran I told when I first came home from *over there*. I had the galleonmaster put me ashore there. That was Master Tor Chancery. The fleet was going to pick me up when they swung past again, but they were becalmed, and a rainbow man called Foss Chancery came to fetch me. Just as well, because I was going crazy with no one to talk to. I'd never expected to be there so long, alone."

"You've had an adventurous life, my dolphin."

"I have. I find it difficult to believe, sometimes. A lot of it seems like a dream. Mind you, some of the adventures, I could have done without." She smiled. "And I'm having another one right now—spending time on another mysterious island, but this time, I'm not alone. So, what else does this place have to offer us?"

Matin said, "There are more empty buildings that way, but do you feel up to a walk up to the cliffs?"

"There are cliffs?"

"Yes, although they're obviously not high."

"Ooh! Where?"

"This way." They started walking again, through some acacia scrub and up a slope which gradually shed its vegetation load to reveal a small crag of pink granite.

Tamzin crouched to examine the rock. "This is wonderful . . . look at that colour. I could make some marvellous pigment with it."

"I'm sure you will, but you might like to look out at the view rather than down at your feet."

Tamzin picked up a piece of the granite and slipped it into her pocket as she rose to her feet. "What view?"

"A few more steps," he said, reaching out as if to point.

They climbed, hand-in-hand, and suddenly they were on the edge of the world.

Tamzin gazed out speechlessly at the vista that opened out before her. A seersucker sea burned blue, close enough for spray from the waves to touch her lips, and in the middle distance, she saw a chain of jewel-bright islands.

"That's not the Star Pin archipelago," she said, although she wasn't sure. The islands looked too small, and surely they were too close together. A break in the blue snapped her gaze to the left, where a sleek grey shape spun and leaped, dancing between air and water.

"Oh." The word came out in a breath. She watched the dolphin leap again, rolling in the air as easily as it might roll in water. "That's what the Black Douglas does," she observed.

Matin put his arms around her and rested his chin on her hair. "Trust you to say something like that, my darling dolphin."

She went on contemplating the magical scene. "Where are we?" she asked, presently.

"Where do you think?"

"I *think* this can't be *my* world."

"Of course it is. Your world is the one you choose to claim."

"I choose the world with you in it, forever and always."

He went on holding her. "Have I ever told you how beautiful you look in that green gown? It lights you up the way other clothing doesn't . . . not even your ballgown. It's so *you*. You had it on the first day I ever saw you—not at Macquarie Bay, but the day you came back to the house in Sydney. You were shining, lit up like a lantern until you saw me in the SUV. All the joy drained out of you. You were so beautiful and so sad it hurt. You were wearing it again at *Wildwood*."

"How do you know? You'd gone into the music studio. I changed while Otto got me a sandwich. Then we went straight to the tor."

"Do you think I didn't watch you leave?"

I wish you'd said something. She didn't say it aloud. That had not been their time.

Instead she said, "If you like it so much, why didn't you ever say so before? I've sometimes wondered if there was anything you'd especially like me to wear."

"I've never said so because you bought it to delight another man, and I can't quite forget that."

Tamzin pulled out of his grasp and turned to face him, blotting out the spectacular view. "But I didn't!"

"You have a right to be angry with me, since you didn't know I existed back when you bought it for him."

"I'm not angry. I'm making a point. I did not buy it to please Dequan, or anyone except myself. He never mentioned, or cared, what I wore. I bought this dress because I was obsessed with elves, and it looked the way I thought elves would look. It felt like mine as soon as I saw it!"

She saw him relax a little. He said, "Where did you get it?"

"A little boutique called *Fairings,* somewhere in Sydney. I can't remember where. Ada promised to take me shopping for a dress to wear to the formal, but she kept putting it off. It got later and later until it was *the day.* She had a meeting at work, but she said she'd be back by four and we'd go shopping then. She wasn't back by four. That was so unlike her. Usually, when she said something would happen, it happened. This time, she must have known we were about to move. She probably didn't want money spent on a dress I might never get to wear.

"When she didn't come back, I went shopping on my own — caught a train to the CBD and walked from there. I turned into a small alley or lane, and I saw this dress in the window."

"So you bought it."

"Yes. The owner was a woman dressed in purple. She was just about to close the shop, but she let me in. She gave me a special price because it was the only green dress she had in stock, and because I didn't hold her up for more than a few minutes. I didn't even wait to try it on." She broke off. "How could I buy a dress and not even try it on? It doesn't even have a size! I must have been crazy."

Matin laughed. "Of course it would fit!"

"Why *of course?*"

"It's charmed, that's why. Your shop woman knew exactly what she was doing when she sold you this. Was she an elf?"

"I don't know. Maybe. Even though Dequan had explained to me about elves, I didn't expect to find one keeping a Sydney boutique." She added, "This dress was almost the only thing I brought to Macquarie Bay. I had to smuggle it into the case." She turned her attention back to the view where dolphins continued to leap and play. "But there are no island groups like this so close to Sydney. What are they called and how is this possible?"

"They're known as the Charm Line, and they're possible because we came through the gateway."

"What? When?"

"I opened it while you were checking out the granite."

"And you never said!"

"You did know there's a gate here."

Tamzin contemplated the sea, then took a couple of steps forward to look down the small cliff face.

Matin caught her around the waist. "Don't fall, my lovely. There are seamen in these waters."

She thought of Trond, the old seaman who had traded paper for a kiss on Dawn Island, and who had sent his great-granddaughter to her rescue when it seemed likely she'd miss her rendezvous with the fleet. "They'd rescue me if I fell."

"Certainly, but you might find yourself paying an unscheduled visit to someone's lair for a game of forfeits."

"In that case, I won't risk it. I don't want to play forfeits with anyone but you." She stepped back against him. "Wait— once upon a time, you told me no one *over here* would ever coerce me against my will. Was that a fib?"

He hesitated. "Not exactly. It was almost entirely true. It didn't necessarily cover seamen, but I had no reason to believe you'd meet any. *I* never had—then."

"I did meet one!" She told him about Trond. "He was mourning his wife . . . but he still had *it*, if you know what I mean."

As well as an enormous todger.

14

"I know. I saw his portrait in your collection."

"He was perfectly appropriate, but I could see he must have been a handful when he was younger."

"Handful or not, *no* is still a viable answer."

"Fair enough. How do the fay goats get through the gate if it opens here?"

"There's a pathway up through the caves." He swept his arm out. "This is how the galleon *Delphinium* came to run aground. There was a bull tide, and she washed up hard through the gate."

"I didn't think that was possible."

"Neither did they. At that time, the gate was not visible from this side."

"I suppose it's like the Fiddle Bay gate—if you stepped through from the meadow without knowing it comes out in the cave, you could get a nasty shock."

"It can be alarming even if you do know," he reminded.

"So, a ship sailing in open ocean hit rocks and broke up. Did many of the crew drown?"

"I don't know the details, but since the folk were galleon-fee, losing their galleon was a heavy matter."

"It would be, since they don't leave their ships. I suppose that's why the current owner doesn't want to live in the house."

"Exactly. The folk married out quietly, but Mistress Ondine is a direct seventh generation descendent of the master of *Delphinium*, and she is about to go through a *ship betrothal* with a lad from the golden fleet."

Tamzin looked up at him. "Arne was going to wed a maid from that fleet—Viviana Dorada."

"That's right, I'd forgotten you had a galleonfee man in your posy of swains."

"I didn't *have* him. I just borrowed him for a little bit. Like Fou."

Matin gave a shout of laughter and hugged her, swinging her up and out into the air so her feet cleared the cliff.

Tamzin squealed, but the hint of danger thrilled her, and when he set her down she said, urgently, "Do you think you can manage a rise?"

"For you, anything!"

She hitched up her skirts. "No knickers? You forgot to conjure my knickers?"

"Oops," he said.

"Wait—I put them on, before!"

He managed a guilty look, but his sparkling eyes belied that.

"Oops."

"You *un*-conjured my knickers."

"There's no such word."

"There is now. Drop your pants."

Chapter Three: Gifts

Tamzin Herrick, Delphinium Island, Christmas Morning 2019

Instead of conjuring the pants off as usual, Matin undid the toggle and let them fall to his ankles.

"Better get them right off. We don't want to fall over the cliff."

He kicked them free.

Tamzin rose on the toe of one shoe, raised her leg and hooked it around his. "Lift me?"

He lifted her easily and held her while she squirmed into position with her legs wrapped around his hips.

"Ready?"

"Ready." He brought his lips to hers and they kissed, moving in concert until Tamzin felt the first flutters deep within her. This was usually the signal for her to remind him to hold, but after the night they'd had, she thought the stable door might as well do as it would. She grasped him with arms and legs, kissing and moaning until he shuddered.

Breathing great gulps of air, they stayed entwined with Tamzin's hair and her green skirts fluttering in the wind.

"Well played, master and mistress!" The voice that hailed them was clearly appreciative and faintly ironic.

Tamzin gasped and looked over her shoulder.

Down in the water, a few metres out from the base of the cliff, she saw a figure bobbing on the waves. His face and hair were greenish silver, so he seemed a part of the ocean.

He said, "I heard your endeavours and almost spurted

myself senseless. Never have I swelled so great and blown so hard! Care to—" His voice cut off in bubbles as he vanished abruptly under the waves.

Tamzin went on staring, frozen, until he burst up and out, leaping as high as any dolphin. His silver-green hide flashed in the sun.

"Care to share—" he began again, but a slim arm shot up and grasped his ankle, pulling him ungracefully out of his leap.

A green-haired maid rose and pounced, pressing him under with both hands on his shoulders. They both vanished.

Tamzin unlaced her legs and slid down to stand in front of Matin. "*Bleddy hell!* What on earth was that?"

Matin chuckled. "I told you there were seamen in these waters."

"Seamen . . . one of them was a girl."

"His wife, I suspect, from the shell belt she had on."

"You said you'd never seen one before."

"I hadn't when I first met you."

"Why was his wife trying to drown him?"

"A little punishment for the waste of a good spurt in the sea?"

"That's right . . ." She remembered old Trond speaking longingly of his lost Gudrun's powerful slap.

"She's probably applying herself right now to make sure he doesn't ever do it again." He added, "Let's go back to the house. If those two start up too close they might trigger us again."

"Ooh! Really?"

Matin kissed her nose. "If they were waterfolk they would, so I expect seamen are the same—or worse."

"I don't mind."

"You're insatiable, mistress. I thought you'd be tired and maybe a bit sore and pensive after last night. Instead—"

"Instead, I'm all excited. Does that make me perverse?"

"Just a little bit kinky."

"I want to throw you down and suck your balls until you beg for me to stop."

He cocked an eyebrow. "And?"

"Then I'll sit on you and — " She broke off with an involuntary yawn. "I'd probably go to sleep, and you'd have to finish on your own."

He stepped back into his pants. "Before we go back through the gate, I want to give you your Christmas present."

"I thought you just had," Tamzin said.

"That is a gift we give to one another. This one is from me to you. It's nothing big."

Tamzin sensed this was not the moment to make a quip about *big,* so she kept silence.

"Do you remember when I asked you to take off the pendant you had for your man whenever we made love?"

"Yes. I never wear it now, but you might as well know, I have it right here."

His gaze went to her neck, where she had once worn a rose, and later, the orris stone disc.

"No, I keep it in my spy-heeled shoe. That's the best way of making sure I don't lose it, but also don't have to think of taking it off when we—how did you put it? Gift ourselves to one another."

Matin looked thoughtfully at her feet. "We just did, and you have your shoes on."

Tamzin screwed up her face.

Matin said, "I'm glad you still have it, because you *are* going to give it to him one day."

"I am?"

"As surely as you are going to find those parents of yours and they *are* going to explain themselves. I don't have the *sight,* but I'll do whatever is in my power to make it happen."

She nodded, never doubting him. Matin was her darling and her delight, but he had a streak of steel in his character than made her trust his word implicitly.

"I've wanted to give you something perfect to hang on your cord instead, but when I couldn't find anything suitable, I made you this." He drew a small, soft bag out of his tunic pouch, and held it out to her. "Merry Christmas, my darling dolphin." He kissed her tenderly.

Tamzin took the silky bag. "I have something for you, too." She delved in her pocket. "Merry Christmas, Matin. This is a work in progress, but I wanted you to have volume one today." She handed him a palm-sized book. "Nell Andover is a bookbinder among her other talents," she said. "She taught me how . . . and you might as well know, Daylight inspired me when she said *she* was writing a book."

Matin took the small book and read the title. "*Matin and Tamzin – a Love Story.*"

"It's sketches of us, done like court miniatures," she said.

He turned pages, slowly, and Tamzin watched the shifting array of emotions play over his face.

"Whenever did you find the time to do these?" he asked.

"I started with the one I did of you when I was on Stella Orris. That was little because I was short of paper, so I made the others in the same scale. Every time I find a new reason to love you, I add another one. Close it up, now. I want to open mine."

He closed the book and raised it to his lips. "I'll treasure this forever, as I treasure you."

"You said once that you had no one to treasure."

"That was true – then. It will never be true again."

Tamzin slipped her fingers into the cloth bag. She touched something smooth and hard, and pulled it out. She gave a yelp of delight. "Oh, Matin – it's perfect! I didn't know you could carve!"

"Neither did I," he said, laughing. "Mind you, I took a few

lessons from Dad."

The pendant was light brown with a fine grain running through it. It was carved in the shape of a leaping dolphin with the dorsal fin worked into a ring for hanging.

Tamzin, fizzing with happiness, promptly took off her shoe, swivelled the spy-heel and lifted out the braided cord which she kept in there with the orris stone disc. She threaded the dolphin into the cord, unsurprised when it balanced exactly.

"Put it on for me?"

He did so, lifting aside her hair and kissing the nape of her neck. "Merry Christmas, my heart."

Tamzin ran her fingers over the graceful shape, no bigger than the top joint of her finger. "Did you do this by hand?"

"Yes. No doubt some artists can conjure, but I'm no artist, so I did it the slow way." He turned her and put his hands on her shoulders. "It's made from apple wood. I know you were sad when your tree came down in the storm, and I thought you might like to have a reminder that loss can sometimes be transformed." He kissed her nose. "And now, I think it's time for lunch. All this emotion is making me weak at the knees."

Tamzin, torn between joy and sorrow, surprised herself with a giggle. "I think you'll find it's all the *other* activity affecting your knees. Shall we take the next round lying down?"

Matin said, "Surprise me."

Back at the house, Tamzin made tea and unpacked the Christmas picnic she had packed on ice back at Fiddler's Rest. They ate sitting on a mat in a circular room where the light washed down through a heavy skylight that diffused the sun to a gentle glow.

"I love this place," Tamzin said, pushing a fresh fig into Matin's mouth.

"It does have a unique charm," he mumbled, chewing.

"Unique in the proper sense of the word. This place is on the boundary between *over here* and *over there*. I can see why Mistress Ondine doesn't want to sell, even if she's away on a galleon."

Matin bit into another fig. "When we've finished here, shall we have a nap before we plant those fruit trees?"

"If you like, but won't the owner mind if we start messing with her garden?"

"No. In fact, it was her idea."

"What, to use her Christmas tenants as unpaid gardeners?" Tamzin quipped.

"Quite the opposite."

"You're being cryptic and concealing information. I think you'd better explain yourself."

He chewed silently.

"Master Campania! Admit it. We're not here just to negotiate the Hot without having folk call the police to see who's yelling, are we?"

He swallowed and bit his lip. Then he said, "We can be, if that's what you want. I admit it was good to be able to groan and roar when I needed to without having to maintain a glamour of silence."

"You did roar when I applied the ice to your cock," Tamzin said with relish.

He gave a mock shudder. "You did that. Why?"

"I had the ice. Seemed a pity to waste it. Besides, icing is recommended for swollen appendages, and you, Master Campania, had a swollen appendage." Tamzin gave him a sweet smile and continued, "But what *you* want is to live here—to lease the island and move into the house. Am I right?"

"It's just an idea. We discussed finding a place to live," he said.

"But this is just as far from *Wildwood* as we'd be at Fiddle

Bay."

"Not a problem if I start up on my own." He leaned forward. "Tamzin, I have contacts in the business, and so do you, although yours are festival related. You know we discussed recording some of your fiddle music. We've had that on the backburner for far too long!"

"Ye-es . . . but I'm no songwriter." She was thinking of *Courtesan,* the indie duo she followed devotedly. Court Leopold, the courtfolk tenor, wrote most of their music, occasionally in collaboration with his young wife, Tansy, or with his singing partner Jordana Dane. She had played three guest spots now with *Courtesan,* always leprechaun fiddle music, since that was what she knew best.

"You wouldn't need to write songs, though. Think of all the music you learned *over there* – what you play on your guest sets."

Tamzin thought. "Some of the tunes are the same on both sides of the gates, but some of them have never made the transition."

"That may be because they're sung by folk who can't *pass.* Your leppy fiddle tunes, for example. I remember your friend Jordana saying she'd never heard that piece you played on your first set with them. And what about the galleonfee whistle songs? They can be played on a fiddle."

Zandie – Nanny Lu loves you.

Stay with Geenie!

She jumped, realising Matin was watching her. The flashbacks she'd had since Zennor used *influence* on her were sometimes disturbing.

She said, "I see what you mean. I've never heard some of Master Treelove's tunes anywhere else. Even the gossoons at *Balla Cloiche* didn't know them, and they knew just about everything. We couldn't survive on just my playing though, even if I did solo gigs at festivals."

"No, but there are others who play, and folk who would

love to record but who don't have the equipment or the knowledge."

"And you do."

"I have the knowledge. As for equipment, Terry is upgrading in the new year, and I think he'd cut me a good deal on the older stuff. We wouldn't be in direct competition with *Wildwood* — more niche market. We'd need electricity, of course."

"This island would be marvellous for musical camps or workshops," Tamzin said.

"Or a summer festival. Would you enjoy crafting one of your own, my dolphin?"

Tamzin pictured it. She had been going to festivals for a year and a half, and she loved them, but she had spotted matters that could be better managed. Those long queues for often sub-standard food . . . a lack of rooms for those who didn't want to camp.

"We don't have the facilities for that."

"Not yet, no."

"It would cost a lot to get the infrastructure done."

He inclined his head. "Things can be managed. We manage them *over there*."

"And you know a lot of fay on both sides of the gates," she said.

"I do. You have useful contacts outside the music world. Branok St Ives, and Mistress Pengellis. Not to speak of your Dames with Dogs."

Tamzin nodded. The Dames with Dogs could accomplish practically anything, and their members covered a wide range of disciplines and interests.

Matin said, "Then there's your other area of expertise — *Elf-Made Art*. You might hold festivals of painting, or creation . . ."

"I want to make a mosaic," she said, without

premeditation. "That seaman in the water was so — so — "

"Well-endowed," he said.

She giggled. "He was, wasn't he? He had an enormous todger. But, part of the scene, I was going to say. He was one with the water. Trond, the other one I met, was up on a dock mending nets."

"Art and music," he said. "They're made for one another. They're pure *you*."

"Dolphins and fairy islands," Tamzin said. "Is it possible to get to those islands we saw?"

"It would be if we use a small boat. I doubt if they're in-habited."

Tamzin remembered the dancing dinghy she had sailed in when Foss Chancery took her off Stella Orris. "Our own magic place," she said. She looked him in the eye. "You really want to do this. It's not just a dream, or a vague idea. You *want* this whole package."

"I do, but I want you more. If it's not something you love the thought of, then I will gladly put it aside and never think of it again."

"Don't promise what you can't deliver," she said.

"Never *speak* of it again, and dismiss it if it ever slips to mind," he amended.

Whole or not at all . . .

Tamzin said, "You'd sell the flat?"

"Yes. It's not big, or luxurious, but it's in a good area. I might sell it to Terry, so he can use it for *Wildwood* staff as well as the office flat."

Now came the big question. Matin had lived at the flat for years, but as far as she knew, he had no emotional attachment to the place. It was a bachelor flat, handy to his workplace, but he hadn't made any personal statement in it. She thought he used it more as a pied-à-terre, while apparently thinking of his room at Bellflower Cottage as a place to express himself. She thought he'd gone there routinely for weekends and evenings before they'd met again when Daylight summoned him to sub for Garret as a model for *Banbury Cross*.

She, on the other hand, had found the first reliable and permanent-seeming home she'd ever had in Fiddler's Rest, and her attachment to it ran deep. She kept her tone neutral as she asked, "What about Fiddler's Rest? I have no idea what that's worth, since I didn't pay for it in the first place."

"Neither have I, although I expect Master St Ives might know. I have a couple of ideas for that, though."

"Go on."

"I know how much you love it, and I do, too. It's part of our history together. It's where we met again and where we fell in love. It's well-placed, close to Oakengrove, where the festival is, and it's near the line."

She nodded. "I know all that."

"And that makes it a solid investment. How would you feel about renting it out for short stay accommodation? People would pay to have a base during the festival week, or maybe an artist might want to stay there for a month or so."

"Or young fay who need sponsoring—do you think Aunt Mim, or someone like her, would live there and host kids while they find their feet? It might be as well not to mention the gateway to them, because a lady her age might not want to use it."

"Someone like Olivier would be able to," he said.

"Would he want to?"

"I know he gets tired of living with Mum and Dad and rattling around at Misty and Lars' place. If he stayed at Fiddler's Rest for a while, he might pick up some local work."

"He'd be able to go through the gate to see Nessa and the godbrothers," she said.

Her apprehension eased. She wouldn't mind leaving Fiddler's Rest if it need not be sold. Or not yet.

On the other hand, Matin's ideas seemed huge. What if

they failed?

You could say that about anything.

She felt a tingle of excitement. "Tell me one thing," she said. "What's with the fruit trees?"

Matin stretched his long legs out and pulled Tamzin close. "Have you ever heard of tree rule?"

"Yes — when I was living at the grotto Shay told me that if I grew a garden there for seven years then the grotto would be accounted mine as long as I cared to stay."

"You didn't stay, though."

She shrugged. "I had to go, to get Cornelius started on the life he should have rather than treading water with me."

"You know the theory, then. Mistress Ondine has a ship betrothal, and she plans to stay with the fleet for seven years. If she is happy at the end of that time, she will relinquish any claim to Delphinium Island. If she finds the galleonfee life isn't for her, then she will return and *live human.*"

"And the fruit trees are to establish tree rule? But that doesn't apply this side of the gates."

"I know. But that's the way she wants it."

"What would the lease cost for the first three years?"

"One seventh of what we earn, but the money is to be spent on enhancing the property rather than paid to her."

"You've gone into this."

"Yes. I wanted the answers to give you."

"Mistress Ondine would be taking a risk," Tamzin said.

"Master St Ives is to hold the trust for the seven years. He has no power to veto, but he will make annual reports to Mistress Ondine who may choose to terminate the lease if she's displeased."

"That calls for a lot of trust and goodwill on both sides," Tamzin said.

"And also for luck, hard work, and flexibility," Matin reposted.

"Just like a marriage?"

"Exactly like a marriage."

Tamzin's head whirled with possibilities and apprehensions. "Yes," she said at last.

"Yes, to what?"

"Just yes. It sounds so complicated it just *has* to work."

CHAPTER FOUR: NELL

Tamzin Herrick, January, 2020

Elf-Made Art had kept Tamzin busy in the run up to Christmas, as a great many people wanted to treat friends, lovers, and relatives to a piece of custom art at an affordable price. Fiddle Bay was a pleasant place to spend a day or two, so some of them made a weekend of it, staying at Oakengrove and visiting Tamzin in the studio at Fiddler's Rest.

Nell Andover, who had helped her make the *Love Story* book for Matin, had promptly commissioned something similar for herself in January.

"No need for the intimate stuff," she assured Tamzin with a grin. "My man wouldn't thank me for a picture of him with his bits on display, but I know he'd appreciate a record that shows how our lives slot together, even when we're apart."

To facilitate the job, she had her husband, Brian Andover, come to the dog park where they could accidentally-on-purpose encounter Tamzin. He was a tall, laconic man, wearing a rugby T-shirt that showed off muscular arms. He sat down under the tree where Tamzin had had her *influence* session with Zennor St Ives and cracked the top of a stubby.

"Day out with the missus is thirsty work," he said, offering a large hand, cool with condensation, to Tamzin.

"Now, how should I answer that?"

That was Nell's cue to head off to the *Paws a While* van for tea for herself and Tamzin and a stock-based *puppa* for Pepe, her chihuahua.

Pepe declined to go too but scrambled into Brian's lap.

"Use me as a bed, why don't you," he said dryly, but Tamzin saw his free hand come down to fondle the little dog.

"Don't know what we're going to do when Pepe goes where good dogs go," he said. He nodded to Fou, who had settled in a silken hummock in a fold of Tamzin's skirt. "Didn't know you had a dog. Nell said you were the only Dame with Dogs who didn't."

"I haven't," Tamzin said. She added, "Fou's lodging with me while his people are interstate."

Brian said, "He looks at home with you, Elfie. Is that your real name, by the way? I know some of you Dames call Nell Jelly, or Jellybean."

"We all have Dame names, and Elfie is mine. I've known most of the Dames for well over a year, and I still don't know a lot of real first names," Tamzin said.

"Care to tell me the real one?"

"It's Tamzin."

He nodded with seeming approval. "I like that. It suits you."

"It does." She picked up her sketch pad. "Do you mind if I sketch you while we wait for Nell?"

"Be my guest," Brian said, raising his stubby. "I knew Nell was up to something when she got me to come here today. Not that I mind seeing dogs or being drawn, come to that. I've seen the painting of her with Pepe, with that terrible orange skirt whipping up in the wind. Very Marilyn."

He chuckled. "You might as well know I've been to your website for a good poke about. It's informative." He took a swallow of beer. "Especially that *Banbury Cross* piece. I'd love to see the original."

"It's hung in a private house," Tamzin said.

"Inspiring." His mouth tipped up in an impish grin. "Especially since I know the lady who modelled for it. Don't look like that. She's our accountant, and I've only ever seen her with her clothes on."

"How did you recognise her, then?" Tamzin asked. Daylight's face was mostly concealed in the painting.

"Nell told me. Pillow talk. I only mentioned it to you because you obviously know already."

He finished the beer and leaned back on one elbow. "Bonzer weather we're having."

Tamzin assented. As her pencil flew, outlining Brian's pleasant blunt features under his Akubra, she reflected that she'd never actually heard anyone say *bonzer* before. Brian puzzled her. He was so obviously an Aussie bloke in a blue-collar job, who liked his beer and his footy, and a meat pie in the arvo, but it seemed to her this was an image he inhabited . . . or possibly one he had crafted and curated, turning back the clock on fifty years of social development. Wait . . . didn't Nell say he was a sailing nut?

But what do I know . . . and why shouldn't he be exactly what he appears?

"Are you planning to get a dog for yourself when your lodger leaves?" he asked.

"I'd love to have one, but I promised myself I wouldn't go out looking. I'll wait for a dog to come to me."

"Yeah, that's how I got Nell," Brian said.

"Oh?"

"Too right. When Julie—that was my first wife—died, I served the lonely widower sentence. Friends invited me to dinner and introduced me to their wives' cousins and girlfriends and so on. It felt all wrong. Then one day I saw Nell at a music festival. It wasn't my scene—still isn't—but I was doing a delivery there. There's Nell, with her hair all over the place, and that orange skirt blowing up, and a blouse falling off her shoulder. Sexy as hell, and she had no idea. She said something about music, and I said I had a tin ear. I asked which footy team she followed, and she looked at me as if I'd suggested cactus for breakfast. A big girl yelled *Mu-um, I'm going back with Pax for a bit,* and Nell switched round and the blouse fell the rest of the way down her arm.

"I grabbed it and hauled it into place. It was automatic. I don't go about manhandling strange women, but Julie was always coming untucked or unbuttoned." He shrugged. "Nell could have reacted badly, but she just grinned at me and said *thanks.* I suppose she could see I hadn't been thinking. I went on unloading my delivery—never worked slower. Nell bought me a beer. We fell for one another and had a spot of afternoon delight in her van. Over dinner, we found we had next to nothing in common."

"You still got married, though."

"Yeah. We thought of living in sin—that's what we used to call it back in the day—but somehow, we ended up married and not living together all the time. It's like having a holiday romance whenever we get together."

Pepe came suddenly to attention, and Tamzin turned to see Nell heading back, carrying drinks.

She sat down next to Brian. "I didn't get you anything, Bri . . . can go back if you want some coffee."

"No worries. I've got another of these, and that's my lot since I'm going out on the boat." He held up the stubby. "Tell you what though, I could handle some chips. I'll go over the road and get some. Want any?"

"No thanks, love," Nell said.

"Elfie-Tamzin?"

Tamzin shook her head. It was years since she'd had chips, and she flashed back to the time when she'd walked home with Dequan and his cousin, Lucy. He'd treated them and Tamzin had watched Lucy threaten to wipe her greasy fingers down her cousin's pullover. The easy intimacy of family had tugged at her envy.

Have I really not had chips since then?

Apparently not.

Pepe scrambled into Nell's lap and pawed at her arm, insisting on his puppa.

Brian finished his second drink, got up and headed off for the chip shop in a long-legged, confident stride.

Nell gazed after him. "So much for giving you a chance to sketch him. He's such a restless beast."

"I have a couple of studies," Tamzin said. She handed Nell her sketchpad.

"Nailed him," Nell said. "Did he guess that was the purpose of the exercise?"

"I'm afraid so."

"No flies on Bri. Not to worry. I won't say anything, and he won't, but he'll come for another sitting all right, as long as none of us admits to what it is. I'd love to send you out on his boat, but I can't handle the open water, and he wouldn't think it appropriate to take you out alone. Maybe we could have lunch in harbour — or hold on, what if you needed to do some sailing sketches for a project? Oh, who am I kidding. He'd know." She kissed her fingers in her husband's direction.

Tamzin accepted her sketchpad back. "I wouldn't mind doing some sailing pictures. I have some already, but they're from when I was with the fleet."

Nell's eyebrows shot up. "You were in the navy? I'd never have pegged you for being in the military."

"I wasn't."

Nell obviously wanted to know more, but instead she said, "Working on anything big?"

"I'm trying some mosaic work."

"That's new. What's your subject?"

Tamzin looked thoughtfully at her friend. Apart from the erratic Daylight, Nell was the Dame she knew best. They'd travelled together to various concerts and festivals, and Nell had recommended her to several new clients. They enjoyed easy conversation together, but Tamzin had no idea whether Nell had ever had disclosure. At Winterwatch in July, she'd been openly talking about her time *over there*, but Nell had been having supper with her daughter and grandchildren.

As far as she knew, Nell had little knowledge of her past — other than knowing she'd been disappointed in her attempt to reconnect with her old boyfriend and that she was now joyfully betrothed to Matin. Daylight knew far more, but then, Daylight was half-fay herself.

What would she say if I explained about the fleet — the ever-sailing galleons that follow the blue lady wind or the golden current?

"It's not easy to describe," she said cautiously. "You might call it a mythological or fantasy scene . . . a man in the ocean, but he looks like part of the water."

"A merman? Triton?"

"Not exactly. He has legs, not a tail. I'm using sea glass on paint for the mosaic, so it will take a while to source enough of the right shades."

"Sounds interesting. Is it a plate or a jar? Or part of a wall?"

"A kind of plaque, because I need it to be portable," Tamzin said. She added, "I finished the other project I was working on before Christmas just a couple of days ago."

"The one for the gallery in Adelaide?"

"Yes." She felt a faint twist of apprehension. *An Eye for an I,* as she called the painting, was intensely personal. Not even Matin had seen the finished piece, because one of the requirements for the 2020 Vision exhibition was that the canvases must be new, unshown and made specifically for the purpose.

"I'm taking it over for the opening next month."

"You sound nervous," Nell observed.

"I am — a bit."

"No need, surely. These people would never have invited you to exhibit if they hadn't liked your work."

"I keep telling myself that."

"Is your bloke going with you?"

"He's got a lot on just now." She caught herself up and came clean. Unnecessary prevarication was too much of a habit. "I haven't asked him. He knows about the exhibition, obviously."

Nell said, "You're not married yet, but I'm going to give you a gratuitous bit of advice."

"Go ahead."

"Decide *before* you tie the knot just how much *we* and how much *you* and *I* there will be for you two. No matter how much you love one another, you need to know where you stand on the *togetherness* front."

"We do. Remember how I said we'd agreed that I would keep on with festivals and the Dames and my friends . . . but we've decided on a place to live together, and we're planning a kind of joint music and art enterprise, using that as a base."

"I hope you won't be moving too far away," Nell said.

"Not far. Do you know a place called Delphinium Island?"

"Sure, I do. Never been there because it's privately owned, but I know the story. Absentee owner—right?"

"Yes. We're taking a lease on that—three years and an option on another four. After that, we may be in a position to own it if all parties are satisfied."

Nell said, "Well, I never saw that coming! What about your own place?"

"We're either going to put in a tenant or rent it out for short stay accommodation," Tamzin said.

"Fallback position for you?"

"For both of us."

"It all sounds rather—ambitious."

"It is, but Matin has worked at *Wildwood* since he was eighteen, and he's ready for something with a bit more autonomy. And of course, I can run *Elf-Made Art* from there quite easily."

Nell pursed her lips. "You're going to need help."

"We know, and I've already told Matin the Dames have a

perfect network for resources and information. Matin left *Wildwood* as soon as we decided on the lease, but he's on good terms with his ex-boss."

"Sink or swim, eh?"

"We're going to swim, but swimming means we're both busy, and don't get as much time together as we'd like."

"Well, to get back to my original topic, I suggest you try a bit of visualisation. Picture yourself at this exhibition on your own. You'll be free to talk to anyone and to take a conversation off for coffee or whatever. Then picture yourself there with Matin. Is he going to feel like a support and back-stop for you, or like someone you have to keep checking to make sure he's okay?"

Tamzin closed her eyes and pictured the exhibition as Nell had said.

She hadn't finished before Brian returned, accompanied by the smell of chips.

"You've put Elfie to sleep, love," he observed.

"Nonsense," Nell said.

Tamzin opened her eyes.

"She was just visualising the Adelaide exhibition," Nell continued.

Brian grinned at her. "Ah, the old *whether to take the husband along* trick."

He remained standing, and Tamzin perceived he was ready to move on. She saw Nell considering her options, and after a moment, she gave a tiny shrug, tucked Pepe in his sling and put out her hands for Brian to haul her to her feet.

"Pud and I are catching up with Caddy and Dash and Rev at *Paws a While* next Saturday, if you want to come," she said to Tamzin as Brian completed his assistance with a pat on the bottom. "You'll keep," she added, almost under her breath and not, apparently, to Tamzin.

"Bye, Elfie," Brian said. "I'm sure we'll meet again, but if I don't see you before, best of luck with the twenty-twenty."

He knew about that already. Well, he did say he'd been poking about at my website. Maybe that included reading the blog.

Tamzin watched them walk away as she considered Nell's half-invitation. The *Paws a While* café was just down the street from where Dequan Qin lived in Gilchrist. She no longer felt the sting of losing him—how could she when she had her magical elf man to love—but the echo of that pain remained.

I'm bound to meet him sometime, as Matin says. But reconnecting with old friends can be so awkward.

She thought of the other important person she'd left unwillingly behind. She hadn't heard back from Emily Scarborough nee Spatchcock since appraising her old friend of her current name and whereabouts. Nor had she followed up on her promise to let Emily know when she was coming to Adelaide.

I have to do it. I promised, and these days, I keep my promises.

She was still pondering this when someone touched her shoulder.

"Daylight," she said.

CHAPTER FIVE: DAYLIGHT

Tamzin Herrick, January, 2020

"What gave me away?" Her friend used her own hand as a pivot to step around Tamzin and to settle beside her. "You smell of coffee."

"Ah. Right. Who's this, then?" Daylight extended her hand to the Pekingese.

Tamzin explained Fou's provenance again. "You know his owners—one of them, at least. She was at your birthday party when we unveiled *Banbury Cross*."

"She was? Remind me."

"Breezy Barrett. She's fifty or so, and she often wears a cape. Kind of an independent Victorian lady Sherlockian vibe. Her partner's called Clem."

"He-Clem or She-Clem?"

"She-Clem. American, I think, and wears a hat with a curly brim. Breezy's—um—not Dutch, but some kind of European."

"Fay?"

"No." Tamzin hesitated. "Not that I know of, anyway. No *bouquet des fees*. I'm just going by the accent."

"I do know who you mean. She's one of the Dames that keeps herself to herself, though come to think of it I did have a conversation about the club house with her once. Very odd."

"She was at your party."

"Probably a plus-one of one of the other Dames, or of a client. I didn't know half the people who showed up that night.

Those two girls Mull and Zen St Ives had in tow, for example. Never met them before or since. Not likely to, now."

"Maxta, one was called," Tamzin remembered.

"Indeed. Maxta Mahoney—weather presenter on the Seven Show."

"And the other one is Liv Bellover. I did a court portrait of her yorkie."

Daylight nodded. "That's right—on account of her admiring the one of my gorgeous Shelley." She added, "So, you're dog-sitting this pooch for someone you barely know."

"I am. They chose me because I'm a Dame without a dog." Tamzin reached down to run Fou's silky cape through her fingers.

She sat quietly, waiting for Daylight to fill the silence with one of any number of available topics. She also wondered where Daylight's Shelley was. It was unlike her friend to come to the dog park without her terrier.

Eventually, Daylight spoke.

"How did you weather Christmas with your elf man?"

"It was rather wonderful," Tamzin said.

"Obviously, Cam didn't go to the *Pear Tree*."

"How do you know?"

"Garret said he wasn't there. Neither was I, in case you're wondering. It was a pretty wild party this time, by his account. A human woman crashed the orgy and got into the salviation."

"The what? Salvation as in Army?"

"Salviation as in sage cordial. Sounds innocuous, and it is—for elves. Gar wouldn't get me any the time I went with him, because he said he didn't know what it might do to someone half-human and without a drop of genuine elf blood. It had a bizarre effect on this woman and poor old Otto got stuck with trying to control her. She was falling all over him and babbling about his balls." She added dryly, "He has very choice ones, in case you were wondering."

"I expect he has, but I wasn't."

Daylight continued, "Her man turned up and took her away, but all the excitement must have shaken something loose in Otto, because he ended up betrothed to *two* women the next morning."

"How?"

"I assume he said, *will you,* and they said, *hella yes!* That's the way it usually goes. Mind you, he's been having friendlies with them for a long time. He used to have a thing for a Chinese girl at one time, but recently it's been these two. Kim and Charlotte."

Tamzin forbore to ask how Otto was going to marry two women. Bran St Ives had said fay priests would perform non-standard weddings. "I hope they're all very happy," she said.

"I expect they will be. The gals are halflings — well, Kim is. Charlotte's a bit more."

She lapsed into silence for a bit, then said, "So, you and Cam weathered the Hot."

"Yes."

"And?"

Tamzin sighed. "Daylight, I'm not giving you all the details. You know quite well what it's like."

"Yes, though I don't know personally whether Cam is the needy type or the greedy type. Or he might even be the *other* type, although it's not likely."

"I have no idea what you mean."

"No, well, your common or garden elf falls into needy or greedy or somewhere between during the Hot, but the third type is usually one with a mani — you know."

"Like Mull and Zen and their dog-selves?"

"Not exactly. With elves it's generally more — well, do you know Flick Dark? She lives in a cottage *over there* near the castle, but she runs the *Dark Room* café in the city."

Tamzin shook her head.

"Okay, well, Flick's an elf halfling, she manifests as a Christmas angel, and she can give Christmas wishes. She's got a cousin who's a Christmas elf — their version of the Hot is a bit different."

Tamzin said, "Never mind all that. Just take it that Matin and I managed well. And before you ask, the holding, or failing to hold, wasn't an issue, but thank you for the advice anyway. May we talk about something else?"

Daylight sucked in an audible breath. "You're still mad at me."

"Why should I be mad at you?"

"Because I behaved badly — again. I ghosted you."

"Did you? I hadn't noticed."

Daylight flinched.

Whole or not at all.

Tamzin said, "Sorry, that was uncalled for. I was a bit concerned when you didn't answer my messages, or introduce me to your cousin Morgana, but then you *did* send a message to say you were going to sort yourself out, so I assumed you'd be back in touch when you had." She turned to look at her friend. "Let's see — the last time I saw you was last month . . . the day I took custody of Fou, as it happens."

"Huh?"

"I was here at the park with Zen St Ives, and he spotted you over near the *Paws* van. He went to get me some coffee and never came back, so I assumed he'd met up with you and got a better offer. I also assumed you hadn't seen me, or maybe you'd have come over to say *hi*, or sent Zen back to invite me to join you."

Daylight said, "I honestly didn't see you, but I can't swear I'd have come over even if I had. I was with someone, and things got — um — a bit out of hand."

"With Zennor?"

"In the manner of speaking." She held up her hand, the

silver jewellery she habitually wore flashing in the sunlight. "Not the way you're probably thinking, though. Tamzdie, a lot has happened to me over the last few weeks, and I need to tell you about it."

"You don't owe me any explanations."

"I do. We're friends forever, remember?"

The way I was with Emily Spatchcock.

Tamzin pushed the thought away. "I agree. We *are* friends forever, and that means *not* keeping score, or holding grudges, or expecting explanations, or trying to change one another. It's much easier to be friends if we can be happy when we're together and not fret when we're not." She saw Daylight about to dash in with assurances or objections and she held up her hand just as her friend had. "Let's just draw the line in the sand. I'd love to hear the next instalment in the Daylight Robbery soap opera as long as you're not going to regret telling me."

To her relief, Daylight cracked a smile at this reference to the sticker she had on her daffodil-yellow sports car.

"Are you going to tell me whatever it is here?"

"No, I'd rather take it somewhere private. Can you come to my place? For pie?"

"All right. Pie it is. By the way, is Shelley okay?"

"Yes, of course. Why not?"

"She's usually with you when you come to the park."

"She's at home, waiting for her share of the pie."

So you expected to find me here. Did Nell call you?

Daylight got up and held out her hands to assist Tamzin.

Her jewellery flashed again in the sun's rays, dazzling Tamzin's eyes. She blinked, and realised Daylight was staring at her.

"What now?"

"Your necklace."

Tamzin put her hand up to touch the applewood dolphin. "Christmas present from Matin," she said, just in case

Daylight was about to say something cutting. "He carved it out of wood from my apple tree — the one that came down in the storm in November."

"Did I know about that?"

"Maybe not. It was the smaller one, during that big lightning storm. It's all cleared up now. We used some of the timber, and I planted a new tree. This is my promise that nothing really beautiful is ever lost."

"I'm sorry about the tree, but the necklace is beautiful, as you say." Daylight sounded sincere.

"It is. I love it the way I love my betrothal ring. It *means* something. It's *me*."

Daylight smiled. "I like jewellery that means something personal, too."

That seemed odd, coming from a woman who habitually wore half a kilo of silver, but Tamzin let it go. "Are we going straight to your place? If so, I'll follow you."

"Okay." Daylight reached out for her hand and gave it a squeeze. "See you at my place, then."

Daylight was waiting with the kettle already boiling and the microwave whirring when Tamzin tapped on the door and let herself and Fou into the house.

The giant painting, *Banbury Cross*, continued to dominate the place as it had since Daylight's thirty-sixth birthday party just over a year ago. It came to Tamzin that her friend must have had another birthday the month before, and she hadn't thought to send a card, or even a text. If there had been a party, she hadn't been invited.

Whole or not at all. It worked both ways.

She stood looking at the painting with fresh eyes.

Garret Rosebay, Daylight's one-time friend-with-benefits, knelt on a model's throne, wearing nothing but a domino mask and a studded metal halter.

His mouth smiled enigmatically, and just a hint of silky cock showed in the shadows between his legs.

Daylight, bare but for her mask and a great deal of jewellery, sat side-saddle on his back, with one foot braced on her elegant toes and the other hanging free. She held the halter reins in one hand and a riding crop in the other. Her head was flung up and away, showing her face in quarter profile. The light touched her pert breasts and glinted on her rings, bracelets, and chains. She didn't *look* almost thirty-six. Tamzin had thought her not much older than herself.

Daylight came out of the kitchen with Shelley capering at her heels. The terrier spotted Fou and danced a little more avidly.

Fou, usually so placid, came to attention and his button eyes widened.

"They'll be okay. I'll put them in the back room to get acquainted," Daylight said. She clicked her fingers and was suddenly holding two dog dishes, each with a minute piece of cherry pie. She wafted them in the dogs' direction and preceded them through the door.

Tamzin raised her brows as Fou departed in a flounce of silky fringing, without a glance at her or a by-your-leave from Daylight. But then, he was an extremely phlegmatic dog. He'd gone willingly with Tamzin when Breezy handed him over, and in the month that she'd had him, he'd shown no sign of fretting for his owners. Nor had they called or emailed to ask after his wellbeing, which seemed odd, now Tamzin thought of it.

Dames sometimes left their dogs with a trusted fellow Dame, but surely they also left contact details and made frequent check-ins?

She was still musing over that when Daylight came back. "Sit down, Tamzdie. I'll bring ours out here."

Tamzin sat, as instructed. She hoped whatever Daylight

wanted to disclose didn't take too long. She was meeting Matin at the island later. Her insides seemed to liquify as she thought of him. She longed to have him in her arms and in her body, driving her out of her mind while holding her close. She caught her breath.

"Tam?"

She looked up, to see Daylight standing beside her holding a plate of pie and a cup of coffee.

"Oh, sorry."

"You were miles away," Daylight said. "Flashback?"

"No, flash-forward."

Tamzin accepted the plate and nodded for Daylight to set the cup on the low table. "Cherry pie? I thought—"

"You thought I'd never touch the stuff again. So did I, last time we met. Great bogle, was that really the last time?"

"The last time we really talked, anyway," Tamzin said.

"My bad. I mean that sincerely. But as I said, a lot's gone down since then."

Daylight sat opposite her, and bit into her pastry. "Mmm, good. Mama Rosebay is the *best* cook."

Considering the trouble Garret's mother's last pie had caused Garret and Daylight, Tamzin was doubtful about this one, but she supposed Daylight knew what she was about.

"Does this have want-you-so nectar in it?" she asked.

"I expect so. I've acquired a taste for it. That won't bother *you* though. I don't expect Cam needs any extra encouragement to want you." She smiled. "If I were an equal opportunity gal, *I'd* want you, looking the way you do today. Christmas must have been very merry, and that leaping dolphin puts all kinds of *merry* thoughts in my mind."

That wasn't quite the adjective Tamzin would have chosen, but she just smiled back. She knew she was glowing. The *flash-forward* had probably brought a flush to her cheeks.

They ate their pie and drank coffee, and Daylight talked of

this and that, flitting between subjects in her hummingbird fashion. She was her old affectionate self, laughing, jangling her bracelets and helping them both to extra pie.

Then, before Tamzin had time to betray any impatience, Daylight set down her cup and leaned forward.

"Right, I'd better bring you up to speed on what's been happening," she said. "What was the state of play last time we did pie?"

Tamzin looked back. "You'd had a row with Garret because he wouldn't give you a baby, and you'd decided to make a move on Mull and Zen with a view to getting a family underway. You had an idea to invite your cousin Morgana to stay, so you could go out in a foursome and mollify Gill and Bran St Ives with a fullblood pisky minx to make up for you being a halfling. You were going to invite me to meet Morgana, but it didn't happen."

Daylight applauded. "Succinctly put, my sapient friend. Mad notion, wasn't it?"

"No madder than most of your notions," Tamzin riposted.

"Very true. Okay, let's take it from the top. I invited Morgana to stay, as I said, and I let the boys know she was coming. I was straight with them—that I had my fullblood cousin coming and that I hoped we could all go dancing and spend plenty of time together."

Tamzin nodded. Daylight was always straight when she wasn't being devious. Piskies were like that. They automatically sought angles, and Dahlia Pengellis, despite having a human mother she adored, had *thrown hard* to her pisky heritage.

"So, Morgana came, but much later than I expected. When she did make it through, she brought a friend with her. Not a boyfriend, but just a girl she'd shared a flat with in Cornwall, where she'd been living. They'd been sponsor-sisters, and that can be a pretty firm bond. The girl's name is Githa

Camelot, would you believe?"

"Camelot?"

"Yes. From an old pisky family, purebloods back to the fourteenth century, at least. Lovely girl, twenty-five, great figure ... well, the full fay gals are always beautiful." She sounded perfectly cheerful.

"Camelot," Tamzin said again.

"Yes, Camelot. As in King Arthur. Do keep up, Tamzdie. Anyway, they came through the gate system and spent some time with Uncle Temple and Aunt Senara, then they wound up here. I had to get another bed set up and so on. I said I'd show them round. It shouldn't have made a difference, but it did—mostly because they're close friends and I'm just Morgana's cousin, whom she doesn't know very well.

"Githa wanted to see the dog park, which was why we were there that day—I honestly didn't realise you were there, or I might have introduced you to the girls, if Zen hadn't shown up."

Tamzin waved this away. She had a nasty idea of where this was heading.

Daylight twisted a ring on her finger and went on, "Githa wanted to see the park because she's a mutie ... like Zen and Mull. More like Mull, really, because *her* mani self is solid, the way the Black Douglas is, not all moonlight and cobweb, like dear little Demi-dog."

"What kind of dog?" Tamzin asked with interest. She was acquainted with three mani-dogs. The Black Douglas, Mullion St Ives' second self, was an attention-loving black Scottie, who loved showing off his acrobatic skills. Mull's brother, Zennor, manifested a charming but insubstantial little dachshund, whom Tamzin had sketched, winning Zen's devotion in consequence. The third one was Lady Velvet, a dignified black spaniel, who was the second self of the boys' mother, Gillan.

47

It was possible she had met others but hadn't identified them as such.

Daylight said, "I'm glad you asked—would you believe, she's the most beautiful little mini-hound, silvery-grey. Name's Guinevere."

Of course it is.

Tamzin found her mouth open and closed it with a snap.

Daylight gave her a sympathetic look. "You couldn't make it up, could you? I invite my minx of a cousin to sweeten the pot with Bran and Gill, so they won't mind me being on gimme-a-baby terms with their precious lads, and what does *she* do but bring a gorgeous mutie along. Githa is absolutely made to order to charm Gillan—and Bran. Not only is she a pureblood, but she's got a solid dog-self. That makes it nearly a hundred percent certain Gill will get at least *one* grand-puppy . . . in the manner of speaking . . . though mutie-selves don't show up until around the time the main self hits puberty."

"So, Mull and Githa—"

"Not *Mull* . . . Zennor! He took one look at Githa and his todger exploded. Not literally, but he got that stoat-in-the-headlights look, and his hands made that south-wards jerk. He was shaking. That *was* literal. I believe he *whimpered.* And Githa just looked at him and melted in an adoring puddle. He sat down and she crawled into his lap and started licking his chin. Guinevere did, I mean. It was—"

Daylight shook her head, apparently lost for words. "Morgana and I just left them to it. There was no getting any sense out of them until they'd gone and got it out of their systems. There was no way I could let Zennor drive home, though. He wasn't thinking right. I called Mull to come and deal with him. Mull agreed to get him back to their flat. Githa wouldn't leave him, so Mull and Morgana left them to get on with it. They came back to my place to give them some privacy, and we went out dancing at *Lanners.*"

"And?"

Daylight shrugged. "And eventually I came home and put my aging body to bed. Alone. Mull and Morgana came back in the morning, and Mull went very tactfully out to walk Shelley while Morgana broke it to me that Mull was taking her to meet his parents. *For an inspection,* is the way she put it. She seemed to think she'd be the one doing the inspecting."

Tamzin's heart sank. This was every bit as bad as she'd feared. Daylight must be crushed — but it came to her that Daylight's voice, as she recounted this tale, was perfectly calm, and rather amused. There was no harsh edge of hurt.

She risked a look at her friend, who was still twisting the ring on her finger. It flashed sliver, then gold, then silver again.

Odd. Daylight, like most piskies, only ever wore silver . . .

"So — what now? Why aren't you upset? Are you going in for some kind of plural marriage?" she asked.

"What, like Otto and his maids? Hella no! Well, maybe the boys and Morgana and Githa will, although I don't see Zen letting Mull anywhere *near* his woman."

"Then why are you not upset?"

Daylight paused and clasped her hands on the table. "Darling Tam, I asked myself that when Morgana broke the news, but I just — wasn't. I thought it was funny and quite sweet. Morgana's a grand girl. She can stand up to Gillan without being in the least bit offensive, and she'll keep Mull from getting above himself. She's the only person I ever saw who can control the Black Douglas. She says *heel,* and the Douglas falls into lock step with her.

"Githa's like a fairy tale princess — *above* normal concerns. She has a sweet soul, like Zennor, and Demi-dog adores her — and Guinevere. They're perfect for the boys. It's early days yet, but I wouldn't wonder if there won't soon be two more Mistresses St Ives cluttering up the place with a view to making babies. I shall be godmother."

"I see."

"*I* see why you'd think I'd be miffed, but pipe dreams should stay in the pipe. I still think the brothers St Ives are sex on legs, but I can admire them objectively. Maybe I was always in love with the idea of them — or rather, with the idea of myself as *femme fatale* with two gorgeous younger men in my toils. I don't think I ever realised how *much* younger they were until I saw them with Morgana and Githa. I mean, they're even younger than you, and I can give you — what — ten or eleven years?"

Tamzin reached out and put her hand over her friend's. "I'm glad you're not sad about this."

"So am I," a voice said from behind her.

Tamzin turned to see Garret Rosebay looking at her with an apologetic smile. He had his hands in his pockets, and he looked perfectly relaxed. "Greet you, Mistress Tamzin. I'm terribly sorry for the scene I made last time we met. I was well out of order."

Tamzin stared at him, remembering the way he'd hurled a cup of coffee at the wall in the *Wildwood Studio* staff room in the most spectacular meltdown she'd ever seen from any of the fay. *Soul-cold,* Matin had termed it. She'd been afraid for him.

"I'm missing something here."

Daylight said, "I told *you* to stay out of sight, Master Rosebay."

"And I told *you* I was going to do what I darned well liked, mistress." Garret moved around to stand behind Daylight. He bent to put his arms around her, and he rested his chin in her hair. "She didn't notice, then?"

"Not yet. She might've, if you hadn't come thundering out."

"Notice what?" Tamzin asked. She thought *thundering* was

a bit much since Garret walked as softly as a summer cloud.

"This." Daylight unfolded her hands and extended her right one towards Tamzin. "Observe," she said. She extended the other hand as well. "Observe this, too, while you're about it."

Daylight always wore a lot of rings, but she had acquired two new ones that stood out from the others because they weren't wholly silver. The one on her right hand was a double band of silver and gold woven together and decorated with a yellow-gold dahlia bloom and a red gold rose. The one on her left was similar, but without the flowers.

Garret's hands, where they rested on Daylight's breasts, also bore silver and gold rings. He saw Tamzin notice, and he said, dryly, "Mistress Herrick, I would like to introduce you to Mistress Dahlia Rosebay, love of my life, wife of my bosom, and soon to be mother of my child."

Daylight pinched him. "You forgot to mention queen commander in perpetuity of your todger."

"I did not."

Tamzin said, "What was that—that charade just now?"

"Don't be cross, Tamzdie. I wanted to show you I've been straight with Gar. He knows what my plan was and how spectacularly it imploded."

"And he married you anyway."

"I did," Garret said. "Last time I saw you, after that shocking display of self-pity, I told you and Matt I'd go *over there* and sort myself out. So I did. I went to the falls to get a dose of *soul warming* from the waterfolk. And who did I meet there but Mistress Dahlia Pengellis, also sorting herself out in the arms of a lusty water lad."

"He forgot to mention he was up to his balls in a water maid at the time," Daylight said.

"So, once we were both utterly worn out, our waterfolk friends considerately left us to talk," Garret said. "And we did."

"Too fucked-out to do anything else," his wife put in.

"We talked and got things straight . . . then I came back *over here* to work. I had my gal pal in my life again and so I had no more urge to throw coffee cups. I went to the *Pear Tree* for the Hot, as usual, and—"

" . . . and rogered some nice elf maids, and watched Otto getting flustered by a naked human who kept admiring his balls," Daylight said.

Tamzin remembered Daylight dropping Garret into the conversation earlier. At the time, she'd barely noticed, beyond noting they must be on speaking terms again.

Garret said, "And when I was spent, a nice maid named Sasha suggested we might liaise over coffee on Boxing Day. I was about to say, *why not go somewhere now and take this up after a nap*, when I realised I just wanted to talk to Dahlia again, and to tell her about the effect salviation had on the human maid . . . I'd refused to let her have any, you see."

"So, he came here and knocked on my door and fell inside. And I put him to bed and got in with him. And we fucked like bunnies for the rest of the night."

Garret said mildly, "We did nothing of the kind."

"Too true. He was too worn out to do more than twitch. I had to make do with—"

"Dahlia."

"TMI?"

"It always is, with you." He kissed her ear, and Daylight squirmed, reminding Tamzin of the *thing* piskies had about their ears being an erogenous zone.

She blinked.

She's shortened her earring, the way Gill and Bran wear theirs, and I never noticed, any more than I noticed the rings. And artists are supposed to be observant!

Garret continued, "I told her I never wanted to be without her again . . . and I begged her to take me on as her forever so we could make that baby she wanted. I grovelled."

"I think *I* was the one begging and grovelling," Daylight put in.

"That's not how I remember it. And so last week we got betrothed."

"And this week we got married," Daylight said.

Tamzin sighed.

"What's that look for? We'd have invited you to the wedding, but—"

"But we met a teg parson at the castle bridge gateway. He's up from wherever to say the words over the latest trollie of Mistress Joan's line, so we asked if he'd do us too. Mistress Joan and her man stood up as out *siaradwyr cariad*—"

"That's love speaker, a teg thing," Daylight put in. "He sang us into matrimony. It was exceedingly odd and exceedingly thorough. I've never felt so *much* married before."

"You've never been married before," Garret reminded her.

"You know what I mean. I felt it *take*. Like a wish."

"After that, we stood by while the little trollie got his head wet. Somehow or other, we're now godparents," Garret said.

"Shelley was best dog and bridesmaid," Daylight said.

"And if you're wondering why the rush, we did it because we couldn't agree on a date and I thought Dahlia might change her mind," Garret finished.

"We're doing it again in public as soon as we can get organised, but it won't be *very* public," Daylight said.

"Just people from *Wildwood*, and Otto's maids, and you and Matt," Garret said.

"And the St Ives tribe, including Morgana and Githa, and Cousin Daveth and *his* tribe—"

"Must we?"

"Yes. Torf can keep them in order, and besides, we can hold the reception at Dave's suite at Oakengrove."

"We'd better have the rest of our families, then."

"And some Dames, and we'll round up our teg parson again, because he did it so beautifully the first time," Daylight concluded.

Garret added, "And we want you to paint us again, as soon as Daffodil is born."

Daylight said, "I've told you before, we are *not* calling the kid Daffodil!"

"Says the woman who goes by *Dahlia*." Garret cocked his head. Like all elves, he had excellent hearing. "Whatever is Shelley doing?"

"How should I know?" Daylight asked, with such innocence that Tamzin knew she was prevaricating.

Garret released his wife and went unhurriedly to the back room, where Daylight had put Shelley and Fou to get acquainted.

He came out a few seconds later with a peculiar expression.

"What?" Tamzin asked, since Daylight clearly wasn't going to.

"There's a strange dog in there with Shelley."

"That's my lodger, Fou," Tamzin said. "They're okay together, aren't they?"

"That depends on your definition of okay," Garret said. He faced Daylight. "Dahlia, my love, my beauty, my —"

"Queen commander in perpetuity of your todger," Daylight put in helpfully.

Garret scoffed. "Did you not remember why Shelley stayed home today?"

"Well . . ."

"It was to avoid the following of amorous gentleman dogs she attracts at such times. Next question, did you happen to give her . . . and Tamzin's lodger . . . a wee taste of my mother's pie?"

"Well . . ."

Garret turned to Tamzin. "I hope your lodger isn't a high-priced pedigreed dog, because if he is, my wife is up for something stupendous in the way of stud fees, and you, mistress, will probably end up with a gratuitous puppy or two."

Chapter Six: The Magic Fiddle

Tamzin Herrick, January, 2020. Delphinium Island

Matin had set up the equipment he'd purchased from *Wildwood Studio* at Delphinium House. He also sourced some small portable recording devices which he showed to Tamzin one night when she was sleeping over.

She tried to take an intelligent interest, but although the interest was genuine, the intelligence, in this regard, failed her.

Matin soon stopped his enthusiastic detailing of the thing's attributes and gave her a quizzical look. "You have no idea what I'm talking about, have you?"

"Not a lot, no."

"About as much as I have when you start telling me about the benefits of grinding granite."

"You're not an artist — not a visual one, I mean."

"No, but you *are* musical."

She said, "I play by ear."

"So?"

"So, that's not considered properly musical by a lot of people. I used to play in a band called Jam Club at school, but Ms Shackleton did say there was not much future in playing if we didn't learn music theory."

"I'd say that depends on how naturally talented you are. You do know anyone who learns to play *over there* probably learns from someone else, or by ear. There are no recordings because recording equipment won't work. Neither will any playback method, beyond the most crude mechanical ones."

"So?" Tamzin said.

"So you're in an interesting position — you experienced recording in childhood, but when you were developing your music you had no way of recording or playing back what you played. Also, I suppose your knowledge of devices has a large gap."

Tamzin laughed, suddenly. "It is bizarre, isn't it? Your childhood was spent without so much as a CD player, but while I was playing the fiddle with the clan, or for the galleonfee, *you* were working with modern sound equipment."

He nodded, then he said, "Never mind the attributes of these things. The point is, we can take them out and record your playing without having to be in the studio."

"Out on the beach?"

"Yes, or in the garden. We can use natural soundscapes."

"Won't wind get into the microphone?"

"Elf here," he reminded. "I can cast a permeable glamour that will let — "

Tamzin glazed over.

"Listen," Matin said. He plugged things in and adjusted some switches. "Sit down and close your eyes and tell me what you hear."

Tamzin sat down and obeyed. Fou took advantage of her position to scramble into her lap. She wondered what he was thinking. With her eyes closed, she let her mind drift, but slowly a faint twitter of birds became audible. The faintest suggestion of wind in distant trees came next, along with footsteps hushing through fallen leaves. A singing kettle followed, with simmering water and the faint creak of a door. Sparks flew up a chimney. Then came leaves rustling again, and sleepy cicadas. The soundscape faded.

Matin sat beside her. "What did you hear?"

Tamzin opened her eyes. "Sounds. They were familiar but I don't know . . . I hope you're going to tell me."

"Yes. It was one layer of the backing track from a *Courtesan* song."

"The Pledge Unmade," she said.

"That's it."

"How did you get it?"

"I lifted it from a recording. I stripped off the voices and the lute and harp, and this is what's left. I can tell it's not quite electronic, but it's not entirely natural, either. Because I couldn't identify it, I got in touch with *Indichord*. I reminded the producer that we'd met at Winterwatch, and that I was in love with the Eager Elf. He said he remembered me. When I asked about the track, he said he didn't understand it either, but that it comes from something your handsome courtfolk man created.

"Master Dane says it's called a M.A.D.S., which is an acronym for the real name. It's a blend of science and glamour and a few charms he wouldn't—or couldn't—name, and since no one except Master Leopold knows how he made it, it can't be recreated."

"But you just did," Tamzin said.

"No, I just stripped it out. If you took out some stitching from your green dress, it wouldn't show you how it was created."

"No. So?"

"I can't recreate the effect the M.A.D.S. has, but now I know it's possible, I *can* work around it. I wouldn't use the same sounds, but I *can* sample natural sound, of the wind and sea, and dancing feet, and record them electronically. That will give your fiddle playing some grounded virtual reality."

Tamzin said, as she had done about leasing Delphinium House, "You really want to do this."

"I do. I really want an album of yours to be our first major production. It's established music that has never been recorded, and since it's traditional, it's there for anyone to record . . . *but they have to know it.* You do. So—" He leaned forward and took her hands. "What are your favourite tunes from the music of *over there*?"

Tamzin said, "That lullaby you sang to Dickon. And *Damhsa Bainise*—that's the wedding dance I played for Shay. I played it again at the ball I went to with Andy and Bluebell. There's one called *Follow Me.* I used to play that with Master Treelove. It needs two fiddles, though."

"You can do that yourself by combining two tracks."

"*Toss the Tattie, Dance Me Up and Dance Me Down, Shamrock* . . . and there are the galleonfee pieces, which are quite different. They play whistles, generally, but I found out some of them worked with a fiddle. I learned some courtfolk music on Summer Island, too. There's *Silk and Circumstance*, remember, they played it at the ball at Broderie Manor. That's a gorgeous tune."

"There you are, then."

She said, "Would one fiddle be enough?"

"We could experiment and find out. Olivier plays the tin whistle and bodhran, so that might work as backing. Misty has a spinet, too, although I don't know how much she plays these days.

"What I had in mind was making it two continuous tracks, with your playing against the sea sounds for the galleonfee pieces and dancers for the leprechaun music, and maybe get the spinet for the waltz. Aunt Mim is possibly a better bet than Misty. She played with a chamber orchestra when Uncle Rob was alive."

"That all sounds like magic," Tamzin said. She realised how much she'd missed playing since coming home from *over there*. There was nothing preventing her from playing, but the gatherings she attended with the Dames or with her other friends were nothing like the unrestrained ceilidhs she'd been used to. She'd loved her guest sets with *Courtesan*, but these had been brief and sporadic.

"My fiddle's up at Fiddler's Rest," she said.

"Whereabouts?"

"On the foot of the bed."

"Catch!" Matin said. He made a broad gesture and the fiddle landed in Tamzin's arms. Fou shifted aside just in time.

Tamzin settled the instrument under her chin, and she drew the bow across the strings. She intended to play a few bars, but it was half an hour before she laid the fiddle aside.

"Magic," Matin said. "Let's go down to the sand and make a few test recordings."

CHAPTER SEVEN: THE HARVEST HOB

Tamzin Herrick, February, 2020. Delphinium Island, NSW, and The Harvest Hob, Adelaide.

Tamzin was glad she'd chosen to paint her exhibition piece on a moderate canvas. Unlike the super-life-sized *Banbury Cross, An Eye for an I* was small enough to carry under her arm in its applewood frame.

She had completed it in plenty of time, using her own pigments, including some ground up from the pink granite on Delphinium Island, and some new dyeflowers she had discovered on an island in the Charm Line.

She had thought of getting a boat and heading off to the enchanting islands as something that might happen *one day,* but Matin had revealed another of Delphinium Island's secrets—a light-framed sailing dinghy named *Delphie.* "It was Mistress Ondine's when she was a child. I found some references to it in the secret room," he'd explained.

"Do you know how to sail?"

"I do, but of course, once we're through the gateway, we can just *go.*"

"So, we—what? Carry it up to the cliffs and drop it over? What if it lands on that seaman's head?"

"It might knock some manners into him and save his wife the trouble. But no, we conjure it down the path the goats use and launch it at the foot. Mistress Ondine left a map."

Of course she had!

"*You* conjure it," she said wryly. She did see why some fay chose not to disclose their status and bloodlines to purely human or trace fay folk.

And yet, as someone had once pointed out, levels of talent varied wildly in the human realm. What accomplished athletes and acrobats could achieve was as far out of her reach as conjuring.

Within an hour, Tamzin was sitting in *Delphie,* letting the fiddle hymn her delight at being back in her fairyland. She had no fear that salt water would harm the maple wood instrument. A leprechaun pastor had blessed it with holy water and poteen back at Balla Cloiche.

They landed on the nearest island, a green jewel not much bigger than Tamzin's garden at Fiddler's Rest, and they gathered sea down that had washed up in a deep cove.

When they had made a pile of the stuff, Tamzin looked at it longingly. "Do you think we might jump in it? Or maybe I can make it into paper."

"I can think of something better to do with it first," Matin said.

"What about the seaman?"

"He's not here. If he had been, your fiddle music would have drawn him for sure. Seafolk love music, but they don't play fiddles, for obvious reasons."

"What *do* they play? And how do you know, if you never met any?"

"Remember, I said I hadn't met any *then*. That was what — ten years ago? And they play brine flutes, and conches. They must have amazing lungs."

"But they like fiddle music?"

"Why not? I'm sure *you* like piano music, and you don't play it yourself."

"Well, Juliette had a spinet . . . but in that case . . ." Tamzin turned her back on the pile of soft, rustling seaweed strands, raised her arms and let herself flop down. For a second, she lay spreadeagled, gazing up at the impossibly clear sky before Matin landed beside her.

"Undress me!" she said, but he shook his head.

"We might have to make a quick—" He flicked his hand and Tamzin's knickers landed tidily beside her. "Let's see— can you undo the toggle?"

Her hands were already busy. Then she hoisted up her skirts and they came together, laughing.

She was still bubbling with joy when they set off to explore the small island. The dyeflowers were growing in a rocky shelter. They were a colour Tamzin hadn't seen before, even on Summer Island, and she picked some and packed them in *Delphie* before they sailed back to the gateway under the cliffs.

"No seaman," she said as Matin drew down the sail.

"No, and just as well."

"And why would that be, dryfoot?" A familiar green and silver figure merged out of the waves as the seaman hitched up to sit on a half-submerged rock.

"Greet you, master," Matin said, eyeing him warily.

The slanted mother-of-pearl gaze flicked over Matin, dismissing him, and came to rest on Tamzin.

"You play well, my maid."

She looked nervously at Matin.

The seaman nodded. "I heard you, and I would have come to make better our acquaintance—but my lady Meri forbade it. I had to satisfy her many times over, until she finally slept and so now—" He smiled, lazily. "What a pity I spent myself so generously with Meri. I could have made music with you, mistress. You are beautiful."

"I'm *beautifully* betrothed to Matin," Tamzin said, backing away from his rock.

"So, that's his name. It's good enough, for an elf. Might I have yours?"

Tamzin was hesitant to give it, since she still didn't know

much about seamen, but she had already offered Matin's, so she said, "I'm Tamzin. And you?"

"They call me Mariner van der Strand," he said. "And my lady, whom I see heading this way with vengeance in her heart, and drowning on her mind, is called Meribelle."

He glanced back at Matin. "Betrothed or not, Mistress Tamzin, maybe you and I should kiss, to give you something to compare."

"Oh, I've kissed a seaman already."

"Have you?" He leaned forward. "Might I enquire *his* name?"

"He was called Trond, and I met him mending nets on Dawn Island."

"Indeed. I should seek him out. So—"

"Your wife's coming," Tamzin reminded him.

"She is. I love her, even when she offers me her temper. We'll talk more, Mistress Tamzin, who kissed a seaman. Until next time!" He slid off the rock and dived out of sight.

Matin drew a long breath. "I think it's time to be somewhere else, before his wife turns up!"

"So do I!"

Matin pulled *Delphie* between two rocks and wedged the anchor.

"Is he really scared of her do you think?"

"Probably, but I'm sure he wouldn't have it any other way. If he wanted a peaceful life, he could have wed a herdfee lass, or an islander."

"*Do* they, ever? Oh—how silly of me. Trond's great-granddaughter told me her dad was fijordfee."

"They wed out now and again. I have even heard of one who is wed to a courtfolk lady." He took her hand and led her up the path to the top of the cliffs. "Nothing to say about a seaman's kiss?"

"Nothing *to* say. I was just wishing I could paint those two, but I didn't get a good look at her."

He chuckled. "You might paint Master Mariner and his delightful Meri one day. I'm sure he, at least, will want to further our acquaintance."

"I'm already working on that mosaic of him."

"Lucky you got a chance to refresh your memory today, then."

Tamzin nodded, but her mind was already on whether she could dry and render the dyeflowers in time to use some of the pigment on her exhibition picture.

The warm weather and sea breeze that played over Delphinium Island were on her side, and she found the perfect tint for Abbie Stevenson's favourite tutu, something that had been eluding her until then.

She looked the finished panting over once more before swathing it in muslin for the trip to Adelaide. Had she been self-indulgent to make a self-portrait from the prompt? It was undeniably her, wearing the green dress from *Fairings* and her spy-heeled shoes, with her dolphin necklace and betrothal ring, and her fiddle on her back. She was posed between two mirrors, showing her former selves in diminishing perspective.

Was it overly cluttered? Was it misleading to show Thomasine in her ballgown when she'd worn it only once?

She could show nobody until she delivered it to the gallery.

The die was cast, so she picked it up, along with her art case, doubling today as an overnight bag. Inside the bag, hidden in a small compartment, was a second painting, a court portrait of two serious small girls, one of them wearing horseshoe earrings.

Emily had not replied to her letter explaining where she would be staying in Adelaide, but who knew?

"Ready, mistress?"

Matin stood in the doorway of Fiddler's Rest.

"Yes, I think so." Tamzin glanced around. She was leaving for just a few days, but it felt like much more.

Matin held Fou's leash in one hand. He extended his other one to Tamzin and drew her close to his side. "Put your things in the van," he said.

Tamzin complied, watching as Matin buckled Fou into his safety harness. The peke took it all in his stride, as usual, with his boot-button eyes bright above his dark mask.

Tamzin had not heard from Daylight since the revelation of her marriage and Fou's lapse with Shelley, but she was untroubled.

Whole or not at all.

Daylight was no doubt dizzily preparing for her second, public wedding day, and equally no doubt rogering Garret senseless every night.

She had once remarked that she wanted a pisky man because *they have the spice of evil the darling elf boys just don't have.* It seemed to Tamzin that Garret had either developed or revealed a *spice of evil* in consequence.

She knew now that she had not fallen pregnant during the Hot. Maybe Matin had managed to hold after all. She hadn't enquired, and he hadn't mentioned it.

The thought she might not be fertile crossed her mind. As far as she knew, she was the only child Ada and Mister Sinister had ever had . . . if she even was their child.

Maybe she should get a check-up. She'd stayed remarkably healthy since her sojourn *over there,* but Branok St Ives had reminded her of a fay doctor with whom she could discuss the matter frankly.

"You are sure we can have Fou at the Harvest Hob?" she asked, settling her skittering thoughts.

"Certain," Matin said.

"I couldn't get any sense out of the woman I talked to on the phone. She just gabbled at me about tay and courting cake."

"It will be fine," Matin said again. "Misty and Lars stayed there with a miniature pony while they were courting."

"I never knew that!"

He smiled. "Ask Misty about it some time. As I recall, it was in foal, and Lars was in fear it might drop the youngling while they were away."

"Lars is a hob-halfling. Maybe he gets special dispensations in fay establishments."

"My heart, we can claim hob-kin if we need."

"We're not related to Lars, except in by-love."

"However, I am related to Dickon, who is undoubtedly hob-blood. Settle down and get in the van."

Tamzin got in. It was the same van she'd travelled in countless times before. The first time was when, as the helpless and almost hopeless Rochelle Marlowe, she had accepted a lifeline from a young elf man and driven with him from Macquarie Bay to *Wildwood Studio*.

At that time, the van had borne the *Wildwood Studio* logo. Now it belonged to Matin, and he'd had it resprayed. Tamzin had put on the new logo—*Arts in Tune*.

They had discussed several variations on Tamzin's idea of Morning but had finally decided it might be mistaken for a funeral service.

Arts in Tune covered both art and music, and, as Matin pointed out, just about any other string they might add to their bow.

The drive down into the city was uneventful. Matin played some of the recordings he'd made of Tamzin's fiddle music, and Tamzin gazed out the window. Occasionally, she glanced in the rear vision mirror to encounter Fou looking back at her.

"I hope you're going to behave," she told him.

Fou's expression barely changed.

Matin parked the van outside a terrace house near Glebe, and he and Tamzin got themselves and Fou, and their luggage, out onto the footpath.

"You go on to the courtyard. I'll hand the keys to Mistress Joan," he said.

Unlike other gateways Tamzin had used, the castle bridge gate had a hereditary keeper. The current incumbent was Mistress Joan Treadwell, a hob maid who appeared to be in her sixties. She had grey hair, a grandmotherly figure and a penchant for well-cut trousers and pastel pullovers worn over a nice blouse.

Tamzin liked Mistress Joan, but she found her manifestation, a green-faced troll, disconcerting. She waited in the sunny courtyard behind the house.

Presently, Matin came to join her. "Mistress Joan is minding grandbabies, but she said she'll send Trollie to move the van undercover. Are you ready?"

"Trollie?"

"Her man. Edgar."

"Oh. Yes."

"Anyone would think you were nervous, mistress."

"I am," she said.

"Don't be."

He took her case in one hand along with his own, then reached out his free one to her. Tamzin took it, juggling the painting and Fou's leash in the other arm.

Matin reached forward and hooked a spare finger into something Tamzin couldn't see. One step forward, and they were *over there*.

The castle and the bridge that gave the gateway its name were familiar to Tamzin, so she spared them only a glance as they walked up from under the arched bridge.

Fou looked about with more attention, sniffing the unfamiliar scents. Tamzin hadn't brought him through to *over there* before, since she and Matin had been too busy to spend time at Skyside, where Bellflower Cottage dreamed in the meadow.

"I wonder what he's thinking," she said, not for the first time.

"Hard to say, with all that fur. He's a most enigmatic dog."

"That's what he is. Enigmatic. Entirely. Exactly."

"The enigmatic emperor," Matin said.

Tamzin wished they were going to the cottage, where they could make love in the meadow, or catch up with Misty and Lars, or see what progress, if any, Matin's young brother Olivier had made in his courtship of Nessa Tremayne. There would be a new calf, too, and maybe chickens. Bees would be busy in the bedding thyme.

Not today. Tamzin turned to look at Matin. "Which way?"

"Let's see . . . we need to go up the chalk and over a bridge—when we get near Cornfellow Pottery we'll be close. Ready?"

"As I'll ever be."

Holding Matin's hand, Tamzin watched the familiar beauty of *over here* blur around her. The tyranny of distance barely existed in this part of the fay realm, so she was unsurprised when the blur cleared to reveal high downs where chalk showed through the turf. "Pottery's down there," Matin said, pointing to a cluster of buildings. One of them appeared to be a barn, and a man with wheat-fair hair and a voluminous pin-tucked smock who was driving a horse and dray towards it raised a hand.

"Greet ye, master and mistress," he said.

Matin responded with a smile. "We're for the *Harvest Hob*, Master—" He left the greeting dangling.

"Cornfellow, lad, and you'll be?"

"Matin Campania and my lady, Tamzin."

"Aye."

"I knew you were Master Cornfellow, but are you Patrick or Nicholas?" Matin asked.

The man laughed and ran a hand through his thatch of fair hair. He had bright blue eyes and a blunt, good-natured face, which belied a quick intelligence Tamzin saw gleaming through.

"Let's see now, Master Matin, is my good wife called Bess or Ebba? Riddle me that an' I'll tell you whether I be Nick or Pat."

Three blonde young women in their teens popped up from the bed of the wagon where they'd apparently been lying in the hay. They wore dungarees and checked shirts in blue, yellow and red.

Tamzin felt she'd strayed onto a stage setting for a production of *The Farmer's Daughters*.

The girls waved to her, so alike she wondered if they were triplets.

"We're Emma and Danita, and our mam's called Bess—"

"—so this must be our da, Nick," two of them said in tandem.

"Except I'm Winifreda . . . and Tara's here somewhere, and our mam is Ebba but this isn't our da, so he must be Uncle Nick," the third girl said.

A fourth and a fifth head popped up, and two more faces grinned down, showing white teeth in tanned faces. "Tara," one said, "and *he's* Ardal."

"Nay, I'm Pledge," the other one corrected, giving his sister . . . or maybe his cousin . . . a shove.

The man conjured a foaming mug of beer and took a sip. "See what I have to deal with, Master Matin? Wouldn't want one of these scamps for a wife, sithee? Two of 'em have enough years. I'd commend Emma to ye, but she's near on nineteen and so a wee bit long in the tooth."

"Thanks for the courtesy, but I'm well suited with my own maid here," Matin said, laughing. "Can you point us to the gateway, Nick?"

"Behind t' barn, and it lets into the scullery," the man said. "Watch thy step with yon barmaid. She'll have ye out o' your britches, soon as look at ye. She near felled our Sim in the colouring season."

"Thanks." Matin squeezed Tamzin's hand, and they stepped around the barn.

"Is he *real*?" Tamzin asked in wonder.

"Oh, yes. He and Pat are twins, and they wed twins as well, so it's little wonder you think you're seeing double."

"There were *five* of them," Tamzin said.

"Those are only the ones you saw. There are a lot of hobs around these parts—the Cornfellows, Cottmans, Cassidys and Applebees, Trips, Charmings and Simmartins . . . and of course the Haydales."

Tamzin would have thrown up her hands if she hadn't been holding so much. "I bet those clones cause a riot *over there,* she said.

Matin laughed. "They would, if they ever went over past the pub, but I doubt if they do."

"Hobs can *pass,* though. Pud Greenhow certainly does."

"If they want to, they can, most of the time. I shouldn't think the Cornfellow tribe wants to. Don't be fooled by the bucolic act Master Nick put on, or by that vulgar claim about his daughter's age. He's as sharp as they come, but it suits him to play the yokel. You may be sure Emma will wed who she wants, *when* she wants, *if* she wants. Here's the gate—" He reached out again and drew Tamzin and Fou through into a cool, stone-flagged room with large troughs, shelves, and work surfaces.

A young woman with red hair, a mob cap, and a white apron tied over a full gown looked up from a sink where she was scrubbing pots.

Tamzin recognised her easily as a leprechaun colleen. "Road rise, mistress," she said.

The colleen turned to look at her. "And to ye, maid — and your man. Ye'll be Tamzin Herrick and Matin Campania . . . and . . ." She indicated Fou with one soapy hand.

"Fou," Tamzin said.

"Go through to the taproom. Himself out there will book ye in. There's a message for ye, I'm thinking."

"Thanks . . ."

"Sheelagh Chalk, but I go by Applebee since I wed wid him in there at harvest."

Tamzin said, "My friend Nuala told me colleens keep their last names."

"So we do — but I want folk to know him in there is *mine* — elsewise too many look at him wid lustful intent." She added, "Should ye want some privacy, leave the beast with me. I've a sitting room wid a spare basket and a kelpie bitch who likes company."

"Thanks," Matin said. He added, to Tamzin, "I said Fou would be welcome."

"I hope it's *only* company the kelpie bitch likes," Tamzin said, relinquishing the leash into Sheelagh's hand. She had absolutely no doubt the colleen would look after him. "I can't have Fou dropping crossbred litters all over the place."

"I doubt if *he* minds," Matin said.

"Breezy and Clem might!"

"Then they ought to have said so." Matin added, grinning, "Best make sure you don't look at the publican with lustful intent. Sheelagh seems not to like it."

In the taproom, the publican, obviously another hob man, welcomed them and pushed forward an old-fashioned register. Matin signed in for both of them.

Master Applebee, tall, broad, fair, and handsome enough to give some justification to his wife's words, conjured two keys and tossed them thoughtfully. "We have three rooms available. Two are your standard pub rooms. The other's *over there.* It makes no odds to me or to Sheelagh which you take, so it boils down to whether you need electricity."

Matin glanced down at Tamzin. "I think we'll take the non-standard one, master."

"Good choice," the man said. He handed over a key. "Up tha' go. Sheelagh will bring a tray up, but she'll ring first." He caught Tamzin's eye. "Ring the bell pull, Miss Herrick. Your phone won't work in that room. You can make calls from the landing or the taproom." He reached under the bar and fished out a folded piece of paper. "This is for you — I think." He held it out and Tamzin let go of Matin's hand to take it.

Matin carried the bags upstairs to a landing from which two doors debouched. Tamzin looked for the third one. She saw only blank wall, but she was unsurprised when Matin brushed his fingers against it and opened an invisible door into a sunny room. He set the bags inside, took Tamzin's hand and drew her in.

The door closed behind them. From the inside, it looked like an ordinary wooden cottage door.

Tamzin set her swathed painting down on a convenient small table and looked about, seeing an enormous bed heaped with quilts and pillows, a small tub room to the side and a wood stove. Unlit lanterns hung from brackets, and an old copper warming pan lay beside the stove.

She stepped over to the window and drew open the heavy curtains, which were patterned with wheat and lavender.

Beyond, she saw the chalklands, and the Cornfellow holdings, and beyond again, a wrinkled blue sea.

"This is wonderful," she said.

"I can see why Misty and Lars liked it," Matin said. He walked over to the bed. "We'll need a stepladder, almost."

Tamzin came to sit on the quilt. "Springyweed and lavender."

She bounced experimentally.

"Better read your note before we get distracted," Matin said. He conjured his bag open and set out his few belongings.

Tamzin saw he'd brought human clothing, including a shirt with their new logo. "Are you wearing that to the gallery?"

"I'd better. I'm not sure that Adelaide is ready for a man in a tunic. Are you wearing your green dress?"

"Not today. I might put it on for the opening."

She looked down at the folded paper, which had her name printed across the front in an unfamiliar hand.

"Open it," Matin urged.

Tamzin did so and stared at the brief note.

E. Scarborough in the bar at four

"What is it?" Matin asked.

Tamzin said, "This is from my old friend, Emily. That is, she was Jade's friend."

"I remember you wrote to her," he said.

"She's going to be in the bar at four." She shook her head to clear it. "Just that. Not why, or—"

"She's coming to meet you." He put his hands on her shoulders. "That's good news, isn't it?"

"I don't know. What if we have nothing to say to one another?"

"You won't know until you meet," Matin said reasonably. "It's quite likely she doesn't know either. Would you like me to come with you?"

"I would—of course I would! But—maybe we could both go down. She might have brought her husband. If she's alone, could you just come back up? Or—"

"Stop jittering," he said.

"What's the time now?"

Matin indicated a large carved wooden clock. "Seven minutes to."

"*Bleddy hell!* Do I go down now? Or wait?"

"I suggest we go down now and get a drink. Then we'll

play it by ear. Whatever happens, it will be all right."

She swallowed and got up from the bed. "I brought her something just in case I got a chance to see her. I'll put it in my pocket."

She opened her case and extracted the miniature painting. "Let's go."

Matin kissed her brow, then, hand in hand, they left the room and walked down the creaking wooden staircase.

CHAPTER EIGHT: EMILY REVISITED

Tamzin Herrick, February, 2020

There were a few people in the bar, but Tamzin saw no one she knew.

There was a tall, fair woman, but she was probably in her forties. She was sitting with a dark-haired man with a dimple, and she held a baby in the crook of one arm. Two young men leaned on the bar. Four couples came in and occupied one of the tables.

A woman sat in the corner, deep in conversation with an older man. She had short, light brown hair, with a lightning-strike of electric blue at the side. The white-haired man held her hand.

Tamzin stared around while Matin bought drinks. Would she even recognise Emily? In her mind, she saw the solemn face framed by blonde pigtails and swinging horseshoe earrings. She saw her intent expression as she wrote down one of their endless procession of stories for the secret Pony Day project, handing each page across to Tamzin—no, Jade—to illustrate. She always ruled neat squares for the illustrations, and she'd look down with a judicious purse of her lips as if to be sure her effort came up to her high standards, then she'd brush her left pigtail back over her shoulder.

Missus Priestly always smiled when Emily passed in her work. Mister Orange said we could show him the book when it was done.

A woman wearing a sun dress patterned in splashy pinks and purples came in from the street. She looked about as if seeking someone.

"Could that be her?" Matin asked.

Tamzin shook her head. "She's the right age, but Emily wouldn't wear that colour. She always wore blue."

"People change."

That was true, but Jade had heard Emily say vehemently that *pink stinks* too often to believe it would in this case.

Unless she was protesting too much . . . like those people who loudly disdain boy bands such as The Mynas, but who mysteriously know all the lyrics to their lesser tracks.

Matin had ordered hob cider, and Tamzin sipped hers distractedly. It was delicious, but she felt it was wasted on her in her apprehensions.

"What's the time?"

"Never mind that," Matin said. He bent to kiss her cheek. "Shall we sit over there?" He nodded to a table at the back of the room.

Tamzin saw it commanded a view of the door, so she nodded.

They took their drinks to sit under one of the harvest scenes that decorated the walls.

The blonde woman in pink turned to look at the door and beckoned to an older woman who had just entered.

Two couples peeped in, looked about dubiously, and shook their heads before retreating.

"Not their scene," Matin murmured.

"Are many of these people fay?" Tamzin asked.

"She's courtfolk." Matin nodded discreetly towards the couple with the baby. "Her man's not."

"They look happy."

The man reached over to receive the baby from his wife so she could drink her coffee in peace.

"A little maid," Matin said with a smile in his voice.

"How do you know?"

He shrugged. "The same way Master Dane knows his wife

is having a lad, I expect."

"Misty told me the best way to get a baby is to hold an especially lovely one and to wish hard to be *so blessed*," Tamzin said.

Matin's attention snapped towards her, but he said mildly, "*I* always thought the best way was to lie down with someone you love and let things flow with a purpose. Not that I've ever done that."

"I didn't suppose you had. If *you'd* got a baby on someone, you'd be with her instead of with me."

"Maybe that's why I never got a baby on anyone. I was waiting for you."

"If we—"

"*When* we," he corrected. "Unless you are opposed to the idea. If you are, then I'll forget it—I mean, I'll say nothing more."

Tamzin remembered he'd said something similar about the house on Delphinium Island.

She was about to reassure him when the woman with the white-haired man delved in her bag and pulled out a phone. She stared at it for a couple of seconds, tapped out a short message, pressed *send,* and laid the phone next to her glass. She glanced down at it and pursed her lips before lifting a hand and tidying a wisp of hair.

Tamzin got unsteadily to her feet.

"Emily!"

Her phone pinged in her pocket.

Emily Scarborough looked up. Her face quivered before she got carefully out of her chair.

Her companion put his hand on her arm, and she said quickly, "It's okay, Pop."

Tamzin walked over to the table.

The man said, "I'll shift over there, shall I?"

Emily nodded, without taking her gaze off Tamzin. "Jade.

Tamzin, I mean. I didn't recognise you."

"Neither did I, until I saw you do that thing you do."

"What thing?"

Tamzin pursed her lips and lifted a hand to her hair.

Emily laughed nervously. "Sit down."

Tamzin sat. "Thank you for coming."

"I only made up my mind today. Pop said, *what's the worst that can happen, Ems?* And I said, *I might start bawling in public,* and he said, *wouldn't be the first time, kiddo.*"

"Pop?"

"My grandfather. God, you didn't think he was my husband, did you?"

"No. Not that it would matter if he was. I mean, if your husband was that age."

"My husband is a year older than I am. And I didn't tell *him* I was coming here today because he'd have wanted to know everything, and I mightn't feel like letting him. I had to tell someone, though."

"In case I was an axe murderer."

"Or someone else with an agenda. Pop seemed the best bet. He knows when to keep his mouth shut."

Tamzin smiled tentatively. "I really am me."

"Yes, I see that now." Emily flicked at the blue streak in her hair. "The thing is, who exactly is *me*? You, I mean? When I knew you, your name was Jade Eliot. Your mum and mine were friends, and your dad sometimes talked bikes with my dad. Now you say your name is Tamzin Herrick. Changing your surname, I can see — I did it myself — but why change to Tamzin? And what did you mean about Jade not being your real name?"

Tamzin said, "I didn't change it to Tamzin the first time. My parents did. Do you remember when we first moved to Adelaide?"

Emily shook her head. "Not really. I don't think we started

school together, but a few people changed schools when they closed the smaller ones."

"I was nine — I think."

"You think."

"Yes. I've never been sure when I was born, although I know now my original name was Alexandra."

"Another name?"

"You don't know the half of it," Tamzin said. She glanced over at Matin, who was talking to Emily's grandfather.

"Your fiancé?" Emily asked, following her gaze.

"Yes. Matin Campania."

"What does *he* make of all this? Assuming you've told him."

"I've told him everything. He's trying to help me to sort it out. I think I told you in my letter that I'm out of touch with my parents. I haven't seen them since I ran away back in two-thousand-and-ten. I don't know where they are, or what names they're using now, so finding them is difficult. I'm hoping to get hold of them soon, though, so I can find out why they did what they did and put it behind me."

Emily said, "Just how many names have you had?"

Tamzin counted them up on her fingers. "I was Zandie first — Alexandra, I mean. Then I was Angie Blake, then Abbie Stevenson. When I knew you, I was Jade Eliot, then Cleo Browning. After that, I was Tamzin Herrick."

"Which you still are."

"No, I was Rochelle Marlowe for a bit, and that's why I ran away. I changed my name to Thomasine Forest for seven years, but a couple of years ago, I moved back to Sydney and became Tamzin again."

"Why?"

Tamzin spread her hands. "Because it's me. It was the name I had when I was happiest. I had a boyfriend, and I'd become *me*."

"So that's why you never got back in touch with me."

Tamzin knew she was on tricky ground. "I wasn't allowed to contact you, or anyone. Every time we moved, we cut ties with everyone and everything."

"You could have told me you were going. I'd have kept quiet." Emily linked her pointer fingers. "Jade-Emily forever," she said solemnly.

"I know you would. You were the first person I can remember trusting. I mean, I suppose I trusted my parents when I was little, but eventually I had to stop. I never stopped trusting you though. I would have told you like a shot."

"Why didn't you?"

"The first I knew was when my mother picked me up from school, and instead of taking me home, she took me to a place in Langdorf. She said we were having a holiday. While we were there, we went shopping and she got me new clothes and a new case. We checked out in the morning, and someone said, 'There's a message for you, Doctor Browning,' then my father picked us up down by a fruit market in a different car and — we never went home again."

"That's bizarre," Emily said.

"Yes. I remember being angry because my mother wouldn't let me have a sausage at a sausage sizzle while we were heading north. Someone had decided we were vegetarians. I *did* write to you, though. I talked Ada — my mother — into letting me send you a birthday card. I used our code to tell you our new name and new address. Ada promised to take it to the post office."

Emily scrunched her brow. "I never got it. That letter you sent last year was the first I'd heard from you or of you since you left."

"I expect Ada didn't send it. When you didn't answer, I thought you must be angry with me, so I gave up. I should have kept trying."

Emily said, "You should have got crafty."

"Yes. While I was Cleo, I was a Scout for a while. I used to fantasise that you'd join Scouts, and we'd meet up at a jamboree."

"I joined the TRA when I was thirteen, although I didn't actually learn to ride for quite a long time after."

Tamzin looked at the other woman sadly. "I wonder if we would still be friends if I'd managed to keep in touch. Or if we hadn't moved away."

"I don't know. I'm still friends with a few people I was at school with, but it's more like being acquainted. If we meet in the supermarket queue then I say *Hi, Clara,* and she says, *How are you, Emily?* I say, *Fine. How's your mum?* and she says, *Not too good,* then she gets to the checkout and the conversation peters out. Most of my socialising these days is done with people from work, or with my husband's mates and their partners. I talk horses with people from the TRA—Trail Riding Association—but I don't have close friends otherwise. How about you?"

Tamzin thought of her own life.

"I have a network of good friends rather than one close one." She told Emily about the Dames with Dogs, and her surrogate family. "I get on well with Matin's sister. She and her husband breed horses, so maybe—"

"So I must, simply *must* know them?" Emily raised her brows.

Tamzin felt herself blushing.

"Sorry. Tell me their names. I might have heard of them, at least."

"His sister is Mistley Haydale, but we all call her Misty. Her husband is Lars. He's very tall and she's beautiful, so you'd probably remember if you'd met them."

"Ah. They're the people from Hobby Horse Stables. And you're right. She's lovely."

"Yes, that's them."

"Small world," Emily said. "Not that I *know* them, but I do know of them. I've seen them in the TRA magazine and also at an urban farming expo. Anyone else I might know of?"

"There's a family who sort of adopted me—a solicitor and his wife. Branok and Gillan St Ives."

Emily shook her head. Then she said, "Oh, wait—I don't know either of them, but isn't he the person you named as a perpetual contact?"

"That's right."

"Odd name, I thought. Like an actor."

"Branok and Gillan are both Cornish names."

"Ah. I was thinking maybe Welsh. But go on . . ."

"Well, there's my accountant, who is also a friend—she's just married a man who used to work with Matin. Her name's Dahlia."

"That all sounds cosy, but I don't know her, either. I'd remember a person named Dahlia. It was on our short list when we were naming our girls."

Tamzin waited expectantly, but Emily didn't continue, so she said, "I wouldn't call it cosy, but that's what I meant by a network. I also know a lot of people through work."

"You mean your art?" Emily said.

"Yes. I do commissions."

"You might as well know that after you contacted me, I did a bit of stalking—I checked out your website, and your blog. I was trying to decide if you were the person I'd known. There are no photos of you on social media, and your name doesn't appear on the website. It's on your blog, but anyone can write a blog. In fact, I do myself—but I do it under another name. Not because I'm hiding, either—it's a work thing."

Tamzin said, "I'm not hiding now. A lot of my clients call me *Elfie,* so that's the name I have on the site. Calling the blog *The Elves Made Me Do It* ties in with that."

"I was hoping to find some pictures of ponies, or some of the things you used to draw, or even a sketch of someone I know," Emily said pensively.

"I expect you found *Banbury Cross*," Tamzin said.

Emily gave an unexpected giggle. "I did! I looked it over very carefully, but it didn't help me to decide. You weren't into drawing naked fairies back then."

"Fairies?" Tamzin blurted.

Emily frowned. "Aren't they? I thought they were meant to be Shakespearean fairies—not exactly Oberon and Titania, but something like that." She put her hands over her cheeks. "The man in the picture looked a bit like your fiancé, but the woman wasn't you."

"It wasn't Matin, but I can see what you mean. They used to work together."

There was a pause before Emily said, "I know you're here for an exhibition, but how long are you staying?"

"A few days."

"I'd offer to show you about, but that would be silly. You used to live here, and besides—you'll be busy."

"I expect so. What do you do? I know you have daughters, but you said you had friends at work, and you mentioned a work blog."

"I work for the council in one of those jobs that sounds utterly boring if you try to describe it. And I write."

"Books? The way we planned?"

"Not exactly the way we planned, but yes—books. Kids' books, mainly—mysteries set in an urban context."

"What name do you use?"

Emily cleared her throat. "Actually—Emily Jade. The first one, *The Red Code,* came out when I was nineteen. I don't expect you saw it."

"No. I was—away by then."

"Away?"

"I told you I left my parents and went right away. You might say I lived off the grid, first with a community, then later I went out to the islands."

Emily sighed. "And there was I, occasionally fantasising that you'd pick up one of my books and the name would jog your memory . . . The second one is called *The Jade Mystery*, and the third is *Lost Eliot*."

"If I'd ever seen one of the books it *would* have. I'd have bought them from curiosity, if nothing else."

Emily's phone pinged. She glanced down reflexively. "I'd better check this — I left the kids with my gran."

Tamzin looked away politely.

"Just a survey," Emily said after a few moments, "but I'd better go, all the same. I can't pretend to understand any of this, but I hope you find your parents and sort it out."

"So do I," Tamzin said.

"If you do — when you do — would you let me know? You could ring or write — or email. Obviously, don't tell me if it turns out to be sensitive information."

"I won't tell you anything that could put you in danger," Tamzin said.

Emily's eyes widened. "I never thought of that! Do you mean they might be *spies*?"

"That, or under witness protection, or illegal aliens. Or maybe one of them belonged to a crime family, or they kidnapped me as a baby," Tamzin said. "Believe me, I've thought of it all. I've had years to ponder, after all."

"Well, if you *can* tell me, please do. It's fascinating — and don't worry, I won't put it into a book."

Tamzin laughed. "Maybe *I* will though — just for fun."

"On the other hand," Emily said, "there's also a chance you're a total fantasist. That's what Jamie would say, if I told him."

"I understand why you might think so."

"Actually, I don't. I think if you were, you'd come up with something more plausible. Besides, I remember Jade—you—and the way we were. No one changes that much." Emily pushed back her chair and slid her phone into her bag. In the same motion, she palmed something from a zip compartment, hesitated, and held it out to Tamzin. "I've kept this all the time, and this morning, I made a copy. Do you remember class photo day when we were in Year Four? You missed it, and when you came over to my place later, we decided to take our own. I borrowed Mum's camera, and we tried to set the time delay and we took a heap of exposures. We ended up deleting most of them, but this one survived. Pop printed it out for me back then."

Tamzin took the photo. It was crooked, and blurred, but it showed Jade and Emily with their arms around one another. Their free hands were out of focus in the front, but it looked as if they'd linked their fingers.

She stared at it. "You know, this is the first clear photo I've seen of myself from back then. We *had* family photos, like everyone else, I guess, but they were always left behind. May I keep this?"

"Sure. As I said, it's a copy."

Tamzin tucked it into her pocket and took out the tiny painting. "Snap!" she said, and she handed it to her old friend.

Emily opened the little frame and stared. Her lips quivered, and a tear ran down her cheek.

Tamzin found herself tearing up in response. She got up from the table and they hugged spontaneously.

Emily sniffled. "We both had the same idea. Sort of." She said nothing for a few seconds. Finally, she added, "Tamzin, I'm glad we got this chance to catch up. Even if we don't—if we don't keep in touch, it was lovely to see you. You were the best friend I've ever had, and no one can take that away, unless I let them." She kissed Tamzin's cheek, gave her a last squeeze, and turned away. "Ready, Pops?"

The men must have been back to the bar, because they were drinking beers. Emily's grandfather drained his, got up, and shook hands with Matin.

He came over to Emily. "Okay, Ems?"

She nodded.

He turned his gaze on Tamzin. "Hello again, young Eliot. You probably don't remember me, but I was connected with the trail bike club. Knew your dad. Tell him Col Buchanan says hi and remind him he still owes me a tenner he borrowed for petrol."

Tamzin said, "I don't know when I'll see him, or even if, so I'd better pay you back now." She dug in her pocket.

"I make it at least double, counting interest," he said.

"Pop!" Emily sounded scandalised.

Her grandfather's face creased into a grin. "Put that away, Tamzin, or Jade, or whatever your name really is. You don't owe *me* a thing, though I reckon Ems —"

Emily put her hand on his arm. "No, Pop. We're fine. None of this was Tamzin's fault. Thanks for coming with me."

He laughed. "Wouldn't have missed it for the world."

Chapter Nine: Room Service

Tamzin Herrick, February, 2020 The Harvest Hob

"That seemed to go well," Matin said as they went back up the stairs to their room at the Harvest Hob.

"Better than I expected, or had any right to hope," Tamzin said.

"Are you going to see her again?"

"We didn't make any plans, but I did say I'll let her know the rest of the story, if I ever find out."

"You'll find out."

"I hope so. Except—"

"It might be something you don't want to know," he said mildly.

"Yes. And I can't unknow things." She shrugged. "How did you get along with Mister Buchanan?"

"Well enough. He had a few things to say about your father in his Jay Eliot guise. They weren't complimentary. Since he knows the story from your friend's perspective, I asked him questions. It was years ago, but he did a bit of quiet checking after your family failed to come back from holiday. He didn't uncover anything illegal, but he was understandably annoyed on behalf of his daughter and granddaughter because they'd invested in what they had reason to believe was a long-term friendship. Though he did say Janice was an odd fish who blew hot and cold."

"Janice? Ada's name was Annis, then."

"He remembered it with a J."

"I'd never really thought about what happened when we moved on — until we went to Macquarie Bay," Tamzin said. "I remember saying Jezz Finchley and her mum, who lived next door, would think it was very odd when we vanished. Ada said it was all sorted, though. Mister Sinister was feeding them a story about my grandmother being ill. He stayed to pack up the house, so it would have looked like a normal move. Missus Finchley wasn't the sort to ask many questions, but there must be a bit of a trail of outstanding bills and un-answered letters going right back to when it all started."

"Quite likely, but that's so for most businesses," Matin said.

"My clients pay me on time."

"That's probably because you work face-to-face. Would you actually notice if someone paid three instalments but failed to pay the last one?"

"Daylight would. Her accountant's brain always picks up discrepancies."

"Hm. What time do you need to lodge your painting?"

Tamzin shifted gear to consider the reason for her presence in Adelaide. "Any time tomorrow between eight and four. The opening is on Friday."

"Is there anything you particularly wanted to do this even-ing? We could go and look at where you used to live, or have a meal out, or go up Mount Lofty."

"I'd rather stay in, I think. I'll check on Fou, but we could get a takeaway, or room service."

Matin smiled. "I'll deal with dinner while you go and check your lodger."

Fou was ensconced in a charming sitting room that let out onto a porch and a small walled garden. A bubbling fountain flowed into a pottery pool, and the garden was well-supplied with shade.

A red kelpie bitch with impressive eyebrows got up from

her position by the pool to welcome Tamzin with a sniff and a lick, while Fou merely rolled over and displayed his stomach.

This was usually a sign of submission, Tamzin knew, but in Fou's case she suspected it was more a command that he wanted a belly rub. He was probably pleased to see her, but she had the impression he was satisfied with his temporary quarters and current company. He'd been happy at the St Ives house too, she remembered, when Gillan had minded him at Christmas. He seemed contented just about anywhere. Either that made him the best temporary lodger a woman could have, or else he was the oddest.

"Need a wee-walk, Fou?" she asked, having administered the belly rub. The answer was certainly *no*, since he had plenty of grass available.

She sat with him for a while, running his coat through her fingers, and the kelpie settled down companionably beside her.

Matin came to find her. "Everything all right with the emperor, mistress?"

"Isn't it always?"

"Indeed." He stood surveying the dogs was amusement, and said, "He's a very *odd* dog, don't you think?"

"Very," Tamzin said.

"Will you be sorry to hand him back?"

"I will, I think. He's not a great emotional investment, but he's good company, he's handsome to look at, brilliant to draw, and he's nice to cuddle."

"That's not the way you think of me," he said, still standing relaxed.

"No-o. You're good company, handsome to look at, brilliant to draw, and you're *very* nice to cuddle, but my emotional investment in you is off the charts."

He held out his hand. "There is something to say for a dog

who doesn't want to compete for affection."

"Shelley doesn't compete with Garret."

"Exactly. Shelley is a lady."

"Shelley is a hussy, according to Garret," Tamzin said.

Sheelagh Applebee brought up their room service soon after they returned upstairs. She assured them the meal would wait for as long as necessary, that there would be a tray outside the door in the morning, and that Fou would be available whenever they chose to collect him. She declined to give him the kibble Tamzin had brought, saying her homemade stew would be offered instead. She then wished them a very good night and whisked away downstairs in a billow of cambric.

Tamzin watched her depart as she waited for Matin to close the door.

"I wonder how Nuala is," she said.

"Nuala?"

"The colleen I met at *Balla Cloiche*. She sailed with the fleet to Erin a'Fee to choose a husband."

"Did she find one?" Matin asked.

"I expect so. She probably has an apronful of children by now, but I never saw her again to ask. I don't suppose I ever shall."

"Never's a long time, my darling dolphin. You probably thought you'd never see your friend Emily again."

"I didn't, really. I mean, I saw her today, but it wasn't her . . . not the Emily I remember." Tamzin fished the copied photograph out of her pocket and held it out. "This is the way we were, back then."

"I thought you didn't have photos from your childhood?"

"We didn't. *This* one escaped the purge because they — Ada and Mister Sinister — never knew it existed. Even I'd forgotten."

"Score one to Emily, then," Matin said. He looked at the small image a while longer. "Seeing this make me realise again how wonderfully talented you are. You drew yourself as Jade, and this proves the accuracy of your visual memory." He handed it back. "Shall we go to bed now? We can just lie together if you prefer."

She looked at him gratefully. "That would be nice."

"We'll do that, then."

"If you like, but I'd really love to attend to you and maybe administer a bit of discipline to defuse tension."

Matin snapped his fingers, and their clothing vanished. He dived into the big bed and patted the space beside him invitingly.

Tamzin got in. "How soundproof is this place?"

Matin lifted his hands. "Very, but I've laid in a glamour, just in case."

"Good." Tamzin slipped her hands down the bed. "Because I want you face down for a spanking."

"That won't be very loud," he said, flipping over and arranging himself.

"No, but you will be." She swatted him lightly on the bum, traced a path down his flanks and pressed his legs apart.

The second swat brought an indrawn breath, and the third, a muffled groan.

"You can do better than that," she said, reaching down to pinch his balls.

"Ow."

She swatted again.

"Great—" He broke off.

"Are you grinding your teeth?" she asked.

"Yes—" He gasped, but not, apparently, in pain.

"All right, flip over."

He rolled over, and Tamzin examined his upstanding cock in detail. "That's impressive, Master Campania. Almost as impressive as it was during the Hot. Maybe a hot cloth could bring it to peak condition?"

"You don't have one."

"Ah, defiance! I can command you to conjure one."

"It's February, dear heart. I think things are hot enough as it is."

"Let's see." She seized hold of him and gave him a good pulling.

He groaned.

Tamzin carefully straddled him and sat down. "Now, Master Campania, I want you to roar the way you did in the Hot while I take you for every drop you've got."

She expected him to laugh, but his eyes dilated until they were almost all black.

"I might not be able to hold," he said.

"What?"

"You know I warn you if it ever —" His hips shifted, and he groaned. "Oh, great bogle!" He squirmed, panting. "You'd better get off."

"Never mind," she said. She moved against him, and he arched his back, bringing a cry from her.

"Ah—" He closed his eyes, heaved and subsided.

Tamzin saw stars.

When she could focus again, she said, reproachfully, "That wasn't a roar. More of a gargle."

Matin laughed, stroking her back. "I have to be more in command of myself to roar. When you start threatening hot cloths, I lose my mind. Are you going to get off?"

"No. I'm going to stay here until you feel like going for round two."

"That's what you think." He grasped her arms and rolled them over, so she was flat on her back and he was lying over her. "Let's see what some kissing can do."

Tamzin kissed him willingly, locking her legs over his hips, just in case he thought of trying to detach her. Soon the fireworks began again, and she squealed herself hoarse, before falling abruptly asleep.

They ate their dinner quite late and cleaned up in the small tub room before sharing tea and a glazed cake that Matin said was hob courting cake.

"We're a bit beyond courting," she said.

"My dolphin, we'll never be beyond courting—if you mean pleasuring one another and learning new things about one another."

"You're right. I think we should get married, so we can get on with it."

"With—"

"*It*. Being forevers."

"We already are forevers. I warned you, a fay betrothal is every bit as binding as a wedding," he said.

"I know, but I would like to try for a baby, and it would be nice to be married first. Not that it matters if one got started tonight."

"I held," he said.

"It wouldn't matter if you hadn't."

Matin sat up. "Mistress, I would love to have a baby with you, but I would want it to be something we both want, plan, and expect, rather than the result of a moment of carelessness. That's just as true now as it was during the Hot."

"I see."

"I think it would be—" He broke off, settled down and kissed her. "Of course, if you should *command* me to blow with a great good will some day or night, that would be perfect too. It would be intentional, you see."

"Very well, Master Campania. For now, you will *hold*. You will continue to hold until our wedding night, when, I give you fair warning, I will suck your balls until you bellow for mercy and I will command you to blow. *And* . . ." She rapped his breastbone with a closed fist. "I will expect you to roar."

Matin rolled over and pulled her on top of him. "My very commanding love, I'll hold you to that."

CHAPTER TEN: AN EYE FOR AN I

Tamzin Herrick, February, 2020

Tamzin and Matin enjoyed breakfast in their room. They also enjoyed one another, quietly for a change, and Tamzin felt blissfully sated when they descended to check on Fou.

"I think we'll take him with us," Tamzin said, scratching the Pekingese behind his ear. He groaned with pleasure.

"Are dogs allowed at the gallery?"

"I don't know, but maybe you could take him for a walk around the Jacaranda Gardens while I lodge *An Eye for an I*. It's just a couple of blocks from the gallery complex."

"Is the lodgement likely to take long?"

She shrugged. "I don't know. Fou won't give you any trouble, though."

"I'll take the emperor Fou von Chew for a royal progress, and you can give me a call when you're ready to meet us."

Tamzin nodded. As always, she felt odd about the infinitesimal shift in her betrothed's speech pattern when he was dressed in human style clothing. Along with jeans and an *Arts in Tune* polo shirt, he had a mobile phone and a wallet with credit cards, and a glamour to round out the tips of his ears. He looked so human at moments like these . . . but he wasn't.

"I *so* love you," she said without premeditation.

He stepped closer, bringing the sweet scent of freshly harvested peas, and he kissed her until Fou and his new kelpie friend grew bored and went off to lap at the flowing water.

Not human at all.

Matin stepped back, looking bemused. "Where's the emperor?"

Tamzin indicated Fou, whose plume of a tail was just visible beyond the kelpie's hind legs. "Do you have the leash?"

He snapped his fingers. "You do."

Tamzin laughed as the leash snaked over her shoulder. She fastened it to Fou's collar and retrieved her art case from where she'd left it by the door. "Let's go."

The walk to the *Project Twenty-Five Gallery Complex* took around twenty minutes. The *Harvest Hob* was a good distance from where she had lived during her two-and-a-bit years as Jade Eliot, but she found fragments of memories stirring of times she had walked in the city with Ada. There were statues she recalled, her favourite book shop that seemed hardly changed through the intervening years, and even the silhouette of trees in the Jacaranda Gardens Park.

"I remember when the purple petals from those trees blew all down the streets," she said.

She stopped suddenly. "Will you wait with Fou while I go into *Oranges and Lemons?*" She indicated the book shop. "Ada used to let me come in here while she went for a coffee at *Ma Bell's.*" She glanced down the street. "That's not here anymore. It was where that hairdresser is now. This was our favourite shop — Emily's and mine."

Matin nodded assent, and Tamzin crossed the street, seeing the purple flower storm in her memory, blowing in through the door to make a magic path among the bookshelves.

The tinkle of the shop bell chimed *Oranges and Lemons* as she expected, but the elderly man behind the counter wasn't Peter Orange, whom she remembered as young and given to wearing ripped jeans and trainers.

He'd be older now, but she'd hoped he'd remember her.

Hi, Jade — buying today, or just reading the ink off the pages?

And Jonquil Lemon would call, "Don't be silly, Pete. That's

impossible."

And he'd say, "Nothing's impossible for these two."

"Excuse me—"

The man looked up over his glasses.

Not Mister Orange. Nothing like him. An assistant?

"I'm looking for a series of books by a local author. Emily Jade."

"They'll be down there if we've got any," he said, pointing with a pen.

"Thanks."

Tamzin walked down between the displays, and came to a stop before a shelf labelled I—K.

She ran her finger along the bright spines and found three apple-green books with Emily's pen name on them. *The Red Code, Lost Eliot* and *The Pony Picture Club*. It felt so odd, seeing snapshots of her life with Emily turned into books, but what was one more odd thing in her existence? Reflecting that it would have been even stranger had she come upon these books without prior knowledge of them, she carried them to the counter.

"Got some, then," the man said.

Tamzin nodded. "Are Mister Orange and Miss Lemon here?"

"No."

"I used to come into this shop when I was young to buy pony books."

"Before my time. Only bought the place in twenty fifteen."

"I see." She tapped the books as she handed them over. "I know the author. We were at school together."

He rang up the total, accepted payment and asked if she wanted a receipt and a bag.

"Will you be getting the rest of the series in?" she asked, having said no to both offers.

"Depends on what the distributors offer. You can put in a special order."

"I don't live here, so —"

He lost interest. "You can order them in from anywhere or buy online."

Tamzin retreated, struck by a mix of achievement at having acquired the books and disappointment for Emily's sake that a local independent bookseller wasn't making more of an effort for a local author.

Mister Orange and Miss Lemon would have had a big display and invited her in for launches. I wonder why they sold out.

She resolved to buy the rest of the series, and if the books proved as rewarding as she hoped, she would buy other copies for little Dickon Haydale, and maybe for Daylight and Gillan, to be ready for upcoming children.

She opened the first book and turned to the dedication page, hoping to learn the names of Emily's daughters. Emily had not told her. Instead, she saw a message that wrung her heart.

For my once-upon-a-time best friend, Jade. Jade-Emily forever!

She was close to tears as she emerged from the shop to find Matin and Fou standing in the shade cast by the eaves. Matin didn't feel the heat, but Fou, clad in his flowing cloak of fur, was panting.

"I'll get him a drink at the gallery," she said.

"No need." Matin flicked his fingers and drew a small bowl out of the air. A bottle of water materialised in his pocket, and he poured some for Fou.

The dog sniffed it and gave a couple of wags of his arched tail before he fell to lapping.

"Looks like a — what's wrong, mistress?"

Tamzin handed him the book, open at the title page.

"I see," he said.

Her voice wobbled as she said, "We were talking about emotional investment . . ."

"Yes, I do see. Your old friend invested in someone *you* think never existed."

She nodded mutely.

"Jade was real then, though."

She blotted her tears and sniffled. "I'd better not go looking for any more emotional triggers. The shop's changed hands, anyway. Straight to the gallery."

"When the emperor has finished his drink," Matin said.

Fou lapped up every last dribble of water and indicated he was ready to continue.

Matin dismissed the bowl and offered Tamzin the rest of the water.

"No, or I'll be rushing to the loo."

He drained the bottle himself and tucked it back into his pocket. "Shall I conjure the books back to the *Harvest Hob*?"

"Can you?"

"Yes, why not?"

"Our room is *over there,* and you can't conjure through the gates."

He said, "I can send them to the room where Fou was."

She nodded.

The gallery turned out to be a complex of self-contained venues which, as with a cinema complex, could house several exhibitions and displays concurrently.

Tamzin kissed Matin goodbye at the directory area, and she watched him walk away with Fou trotting industriously in his rolling gait towards the Jacaranda Gardens. She half-wished she were going with them, but she made herself focus on the upcoming lodgement.

The directory had arrows and dotted lines, pointing to venues evidently named after famous Australians. *Makellar, Lawson, Paterson, Atkinson, McCubbin, Joyce, Spenser.* The one called *Spenser* was a large central building, with the others arranged around it. The 2020 Vision exhibition was to be hung in the *Paterson* room, so Tamzin followed the red-coded footprints around the hexagonal perimeter.

The outer windows were covered with blinds patterned with newspaper, presumably to keep the public and patrons from seeing the exhibits too early.

Tamzin pressed an intercom and stated her business, and was presently buzzed in.

The large, light room had tall screen partitions turned inwards, making a second layer of secrecy for the paintings.

Tamzin walked down to the end of the room, where a man stood up from a desk to greet her.

"Tamzin Herrick, from *Elf-Made Art*," she said.

The man, dark-haired and clever looking, with a dimple to one side of an expressive mouth, smiled at her warmly. "Welcome, Tamzin. I'm Dan Fanshaw. I'm glad you decided to join the exhibition."

He had a slight English accent, overlaid by an Australian one, and a good deal of presence. He was vaguely familiar, and after a few seconds Tamzin identified him.

"You were in the *Harvest Hob* yesterday."

He lifted his brows. "So I was. It's my local."

"We're staying there," she explained.

"We?" He looked beyond her as if expecting someone else.

"My fiancé and I — and our lodger, Fou. He's a dog, by the way."

Dan Fanshaw's face crinkled into a grin. "I see. Since my family includes a pink and white unicorn who has to be included in all family outings, I empathise. That's down to our daughter, Paola. You wouldn't have seen either of them yesterday. They were at home with a neighbour."

"You had a baby with you."

"Baptista, the fourth and final flower in our posy of daughters. My wife has a son in his twenties, and when he and his wife visit us, they'll bring a horse with them." He shrugged. "Life with my wife is always a trifle *interesting*."

Tamzin recalled that the wife in question was a courtfolk woman. Undoubtedly, Dan Fanshaw knew he was living with *five* fairies, but neither of them mentioned it.

He turned to glance at her case. "You have your painting in there?"

Tamzin assented. She lifted the case easily onto the desk. It was the one Darragh Treelove and Zeph Maple had given to her during the time she lived with the clan at Dancing Tor. It was made of polished maple wood, and it was charmed, so it held a good deal more than seemed possible, and it weighed next to nothing, even when packed.

She undid the lid, which fastened with one of the traditional leprechaun horseshoe clasps, and lifted out the painting.

"It's in a frame, but if you prefer to mount it yourself to make things uniform, I can take it out," she said.

He waved this away. "Uniformity is not our intention. Twenty-twenty Vision is all about pure self-expression, so we prefer the pieces presented by the artists in any way they think fit. My own entry is painted on a hubcap." His face crinkled again. "Yes, I am one of the twenty chosen artists, but it's not vainglory on my part. I was invited by Wayne Ellington, one of the owners." A faint shadow crossed his face, as if the invitation hadn't been an entirely positive experience. Then he rested his hands on the wrapped canvas and said, "You are welcome to hang your picture in any of the blank places. There are nails and brackets and whatever else you need over in the break room. If you need assistance, either I or Wayne can help out."

"I can manage, but don't you need to check the painting first?" Tamzin asked.

"No. We have elected *not* to oversee the placement, so as to keep the pieces absolutely private until the unveiling. It's bizarre, I agree. One of the pieces someone brought in earlier was—um—a rather odd shape, but none of us has any idea what it is. I'm just hoping no one has interpreted the *eye* part of the prompt too literally. Health and Safety might step in if a trip to the butcher was involved."

Tamzin shook her head. Dan Fanshaw had written to her initially, but she hadn't realised he was so talkative. "I do need to lodge this, though?"

"Yes. Come to the computer terminal. You can use your thumbprint as a password. Once you're in the system, you'll be able to access the lodgement forms. Just fill them out. When you're finished, stay logged in, because you'll need to choose a display area, and register the number. Just click *okay* to sign the declaration. All clear?"

It wasn't, especially, but Tamzin said she hoped so.

Her thumbprint was duly recorded, and she began to fill out the form. *Title of work* was easy, as were her name and driver's licence. She used the date of birth Branok St Ives had established for her when he reconnected her to her Tamzin identity after her return from *over there*.

Place of birth was more difficult. Branok had chosen a maternity hospital that had since been demolished. No one had ever questioned this, so Tamzin used it. *Affiliation* was easy—*Elf-Made Art*. She was about to put her Fiddler's Rest address when she changed her mind and put the web address instead. The move to Delphinium Island was a work in progress, and the exhibition was due to run for six months.

Influences brought her up short.

The only formal training she'd had was from August Herron, her visual arts teacher at Diversity High, during her original tenure as Tamzin Herrick. He couldn't be said to have influenced her, though. True, he was an elf man and she'd been painting elves, but she'd begun that before Dequan Qin explained to her that elves were real, and that she already knew some. As she recalled, she'd started spontaneously after a school excursion to Fiddle Bay, where she now lived.

Nanny Lu loves you, Zandie.

The small flashbacks had been happening since Aureate Shale had informed her of her original name. Zen St Ives had used *influence* to help her to find out more, but she didn't have enough information to round out the picture.

I played with elves when I was little. I thought I was one. I danced to leprechaun music over there. Nanny Lu loved me, but I —

She dragged herself back to the present.

In the end, she left that line blank. Surely not everyone admitted to being influenced in their work.

Inspiration.

That was as bad as *influence*, and just as impossible.

Medium.

Natural pigments on canvas, framed in apple wood.

Price.

N/A she typed. She didn't know if she wanted to hang *An Eye for an I* on a wall at her new home, but she didn't want anyone else having it. It was too personal. To sell it would be too much like selling a piece of her soul.

I have not shown this piece or discussed it in detail with anyone else, and to the best of my knowledge no one has seen it.

That was okay too, and she was glad she'd resisted the temptation to show it to Matin.

She left the lodgement open as instructed, and she went to find an appropriate space, down between two of the screens.

The frame was already mounted for hanging, so all she had to do was fasten a bracket to the screen. A blank chalk board waited to be filled in with name, title and medium.

As she did this, memorising the number—nineteen—to add to her lodgement, Tamzin heard someone moving about on the other side of the screen. She assumed it was another artist hanging work. Evidently it was someone Dan Fanshaw knew, because she heard no introductions, but just a casual comment or two about the rate of lodgement.

The back of her neck prickled slightly, as she smelled polish.

Boot polish seemed an odd medium for artwork, but maybe no odder than ground pink granite.

She stood back to look at *An Eye for an I,* trying to see it objectively.

Is that an original way of looking at myself, or am I being precious?

She pulled the white sheet down over her painting, leaving only the chalkboard visible, returned to the terminal, added the final information, and logged out.

"All done, Tamzin?" Dan Fanshaw looked up from the desk.

"Yes. I think so."

"Have you veiled it?"

"I have."

"I'll come with you to seal the veil. We use old-fashioned sealing wax, would you believe? You'll put your thumbprint on it, so it can't be replicated."

Tamzin considered this was going *too* far, but she acquiesced. The sealing wax smelled strong and unfamiliar. Maybe that was what she'd smelled before?

"Are there many more to come?" she asked as she pressed her thumb into the warm wax.

"A few. The grand opening is on Friday. You'll be here for the reveal, I hope. If not, you'll need to nominate a proxy."

"I'll be here."

"I'll look forward to seeing you and your fiancé then. What's his name, by the way? We can pre-approve him."

Tamzin saw no reason not to tell him. "Matin Campania."

"Another artist?"

"He works in music production. We're combining forces as *Arts in Tune.*"

Dan said, "A good combination. I'm not musical in the least, and neither is my wife, but her son is a singer and musician. Gets it from his father, since he certainly didn't get it from Nan. You live in Sydney, right?"

"I'm at Fiddle Bay at present, but we're moving down to Delphinium Island later this year."

"Small world. Nan's son was performing at Fiddle Bay a couple of years back — a festival at Oakengrove. Do you know it?"

"Yes, I've been there quite a few times. My friend Nell and I go around the festival trail, and that was the first one we went to together." She hesitated, putting facts together and linking them to conclusions. "Would your stepson be Court Leopold of *Courtesan*?"

Dan grinned. "He is indeed. How did you work that out?"

"You mentioned him visiting with his wife and a horse, and I saw them at Winterwatch last year — horse and all. I know him slightly — I've played guest sets with them. Besides, he looks like your wife."

"He does indeed. The first time I met Nan I knew she'd never be able to deny him as her son — not that she'd want to, but she looked ridiculously young to have a big boy of fourteen. It's as well he does look like her, as our girls all take after me."

For a moment, Tamzin thought he was going to pull up some family photos on his phone, but he didn't. The intercom buzzed and a female voice called, "Pen Inkersoll — I hope I'm in the right place."

CHAPTER ELEVEN: GHOSTS

Tamzin Herrick, Adelaide, February, 2020

Dan buzzed the woman in and turned aside to run through the same spiel he had given Tamzin.

Tamzin, recognising the name of the newcomer, felt a surge of fannish delight at having her work showcased alongside that of someone she admired. She hoped Pen had elected to draw one of her magical cat pictures with the signature indigo eyes. It seemed likely, given the exhibition theme. On the other hand, she had also illustrated the gorgeous *Orders of the Fay* series Gillan had given her.

She glanced at the other woman as she turned to leave the gallery, seeing her as a tall, dark person, dressed in cream and yellow. She might have been in her late thirties, and she exuded a delight in life Tamzin recognised with fellow feeling. That was the way *she* felt when she was with Matin, and when she painted or played her fiddle.

Two men stood over near the door, one tall with dark blue eyes, and the other wearing a flamboyant hibiscus-print shirt with a matching cap and gazing at his phone. Presumably, one of these men belonged with Pen and was the source of some of her delight. Tamzin's money was on the first man, since he was wrangling a pair of children who looked like Pen.

He's a fairy! The one Gillan said is Andorie Sorenson's nephew.

She almost laughed as his hand moved, almost too fast to see, and a soft toy the wee girl was aiming at her brother appeared under his arm. "Dove . . ."

The child turned a soulful face up to her father. "Daddy, that's not fair."

"Neither is throwing things at your brother."

Pen turned a laughing glance over her shoulder.

Yes, that's her man. No wonder she looks the way she does. He's gorgeous.

Tamzin slid past the group, catching a confusing scent of spring flowers, herbs, and the darker smell she thought was wax or polish. She sneezed.

"I beg your pardon," she murmured.

The little girl turned and focused on her face with disturbing dark blue eyes. "Nice fair—" she began and looked confused. She shook her head.

Well, I do confuse people, Tamzin thought ruefully as she hurried outside.

She was fishing for her phone to alert Matin that she was ready to meet him when she saw him standing by the signs where they had parted half an hour before.

"That was well timed," she said cheerfully. She took his arm, and he bent to kiss her.

"You'll never guess who I just saw," she began, but then she realised her brief encounter wouldn't seem so momentous to Matin. He was probably aware of Pen Inkersoll's *Magic Cat* illustrations, and maybe even of her embellishments for *Orders of the Fay*, but he had never discussed them with her.

"Who?" He looked about.

Tamzin changed tack. "Dan Fanshaw, the person who invited me here, is inside, and guess what—remember the courtfolk woman we saw in the bar yesterday with her man and a baby? He's her husband. And *she's* Court Leopold's mother."

Matin looked distracted. "Oh."

"Court Leopold of *Courtesan*. You know."

"He's here?"

"No, his stepfather is the one—oh, it doesn't matter. Just one of those odd *seven degrees of separation* things. I know someone from going to festivals, and his stepfather is right here, babbling about unicorns and posies of daughters, and advising me on sealing wax."

Matin still looked perplexed.

"You came back early," Tamzin said. "Is everything all right?"

Matin looked around. "Come away from here. People are trying to read the sign."

"Oh." A bit deflated, Tamzin realised he was right. Two tourists wearing high-viz yellow vests, matching bike helmets, and wrap-around visors had just pulled up to the side, apparently waiting for her to move.

Tamzin took a step back and almost tripped as Fou, usually so phlegmatic, barked suddenly and shot around behind her.

She staggered, and Matin grabbed her, losing his grip on the leash.

Fou headed towards the cyclists, one of whom exploded, "*Shite!*" and dropped the bike, thrusting it away from him to fall with a fearful clatter. It landed across Fou's back, and he yelped, squirmed out from underneath and rushed back to Tamzin with his tail tucked low.

She bent to pick him up, flushing with mingled anger and embarrassment.

I ought to apologise for him, but did that idiot have to drop the bike? He's a Pekingese, not a charging rottweiler. What possible harm could he do?

Matin took matters into his own hands and crossed to the couple to have a brief conversation. He helped the man to right his bicycle before he returned to take Tamzin by the arm. He picked up her case, which she had dropped in the confusion, and they headed away from the gallery complex.

"Where are we going?" Tamzin asked, still shaken.

"I think we'll lose ourselves in the Jacaranda Gardens

before anything else happens." He sounded a bit brusque, and Tamzin glanced at him as he hurried them along.

"I'll put Fou down and make sure he's all right."

"Give him to me." He took the dog and they hurried on to enter the wide gates of Jacaranda Gardens.

The famous blue-purple trees weren't in bloom, but there was still plenty to see in the gardens. Tamzin gradually felt less ruffled. She spotted a gazebo mantled in ferns and she drew Matin over to sit in the shade.

He put Fou down, and Tamzin bent to run her hands over the dog's compact little body. He seemed unharmed.

"I'm sorry about that," Matin said.

"*You* didn't drop the bike on him."

"I should have kept a grip on the leash or conjured the bike before it hit."

"It was so sudden."

"I had forewarning. He's been behaving oddly since not long after we left you."

"I hope he hasn't got heat stroke. He's not used to being in such a hot climate."

"He's had water and it's shady here. He just seems unsettled."

"Yes, what was that all about?" Tamzin looked down at her lodger, who sat panting gently. He whined and turned to gaze towards the entry to the gardens. "Fou? I wonder if we ought to get him checked over by a vet."

"That might be difficult in a strange city, unless your friend Emily can help."

Tamzin thought about that. "I don't think he's ill, just being odd. And it's not surprising, after having a bike dropped on him. Did you manage to calm those cyclists down?"

"Yes. The bloke apologised. He wasn't expecting a furball to dash at him, though it didn't look like an attack to me."

"Oh well, no real harm done." Tamzin looked about her.

The gardens were nicely appointed, but the heat shimmer was strong, and she felt the beginnings of a headache. "Do you know what I'd really like to do, Master Campania?"

"What?"

"I'd like us to go back through the gates. We could go to Bellflower Cottage, or just find a pool or a creek to lounge in." She looked at him hopefully.

"What about your exhibition opening?"

"That's on Friday evening. We could be back for that."

Matin brushed her hair away from her brow. "Are you all right, my dolphin?"

"Yes, perfectly. I just don't have anything specific to do between now and again, and I keep half-remembering things and places I must have known when I lived here before as Jade."

"Are you sure that's all it is?"

"Honestly?"

He inclined his head.

"I *think* so. I'm not really part of the art scene at home, because I have my own niche where I'm accepted. Our circle . . . the Dames, the St Ives, your family and my regulars — even Daylight and Garret — keep us insulated because they like and accept us, and we know them."

"Accepting is the thing," he agreed.

"And in return, we accept them. *Whole or not at all,* as you said once to me. You were referring to Daylight and Garret, but it has a wider context. We're just so incredibly lucky, Master Campania."

"I know. I can't count my blessings every day, because I would never get to the end of them."

Tamzin said thoughtfully, "In the gallery, there was a painting on a hubcap and something to do with boot polish. I expect Pen Inkersoll's work will be more accessible, like mine, but . . ." She looked at him helplessly. "I've been having flashbacks, and worlds-colliding sorts of things all day. Ghosts."

"How do you mean?" He secured Fou's leash to the gazebo seat before he took her hand in both of his.

"My favourite band that I stalk with Nell — and even get to play with now and again — and now I met the stepfather of one of the members, who happens to be the one who sent me an invitation to submit for this exhibition. One of my favourite artists, whose work I know from books and prints, turns out to be another person exhibiting here. She has a fairy husband who lights up her life, and I have that — Emily's grown up and writing books that hint at *me*. She referred to me as her *once-upon-a-time friend*. It's echoes of me. If I closed my eyes, I'd see Jade walking along here with Ada, asking for pocket money to buy the last book in the *Riverbiscuit* series, which would finish the puzzle the spines made when they were shelved in order. And being told, *No, but maybe next time . . .* and," she added with a gush of anger, "she knew full well there would be no next time. The *next day* we left Adelaide and my books and my mountain bike and Emily behind."

Matin went on holding her hand, and Tamzin tossed off her mood. "That's enough out of me. I keep *on* reverting to these — these *things* in my past that can't be mended. I could walk back into *Oranges and Lemons* and buy the whole set of *Riverbiscuit,* or order it, since he probably doesn't have them all . . . but would I ever read them?"

"You might, but you should give yourself the chance. You won't even have to buy them."

"No?"

His smile lit up the gazebo. "Mistress Mistley Campania received the whole set from Aunt Mim, back in the day when she was married to Uncle Robert. He knew the author's dad — they were both members of the Odd Gentlemen quartet."

"Oh my God, oh, my *God!*" Tamzin said, torn between

laughter and hysteria.

"So, you ask Misty about borrowing them the next time we get together. Only don't blame me if she bends your ear for hours. One of the reasons she was attracted to Lars was because of his affinity with horses."

"I will! And I might ask if I can go riding with her one day. I never realised she was really interested in horses from childhood, though I know they have a stable."

"Ah, that's because you know Mistress Haydale of Bellflower Cottage. You're not so well acquainted with Missus Haydale of *Hobby Horse Stables*. You might not even recognise her if you encountered her at a gymkhana or an expo." He pulled a solemn face. "Rumour has it she has even been spotted in a puffa vest and riding boots."

"Oh, my God!"

"Besides, it might soothe you to know I have ghosts as well," Matin said quietly. "Not specifically here in Adelaide, as I haven't been here before, but I sometimes see, or smell, or hear something from strangers that makes me think I know them. I think it's just part of life."

"So, I'd better stop being precious and dwelling on things that mean nothing more than odd coincidences," Tamzin said, laughing. "But I would still like to go *over there* for the rest of today and tomorrow if you don't mind. It could be a holiday within a holiday. It would also give Fou a break from the heat, and from whatever's troubling his furry little equilibrium."

"Done," Matin said.

He unhitched Fou's leash from the gazebo and they headed back towards the *Harvest Hob*.

"We can leave our things in the room," Tamzin began. She broke off with a sudden laugh. "Will you look at that! Isn't that bike a bit familiar?"

"I refuse to believe that's the same bike," Matin said.

"Look, the rider has a conspicuous lack of Lycra, but an equally conspicuous floral compulsion."

"Mister Hibiscus. He was at the gallery too, fiddling with his phone," Tamzin said.

CHAPTER TWELVE: UNVEILED

Tamzin Herrick, February, 2020

On Friday, Tamzin and Matin returned through the *Harvest Hob* gate with Fou, who had reverted to his usual placidity.

Tamzin put on her green dress, and Matin again wore his *Arts in Tune* shirt. He'd brought business cards to offer alongside Tamzin's.

They had discussed whether to take Fou to the gallery, but Tamzin had decided he should come along. The evening was cooler, and, as Matin said, he could always take the little dog back to the *Harvest Hob* if necessary.

When they reached the gallery complex, the place was crowded. Glowing lights led to the Paterson Gallery, and Tamzin's way was cleared by the invitation card Dan Fanshaw had left for them at the Hob.

Tamzin Herrick of Elf-Made Art E + Matin Campania of Arts in Tune G, it stated, and the names were on badges pinned to the card. An attached note informed them that E designated an exhibitor while G was for guests.

Matin fastened his badge on. Then he did Tamzin's, looking down at her with such affection she could barely contain her desire to drag his head down for an explicit kiss that might have shocked the gallery patrons.

Excitement ran through her veins, but whether it was due to being with him or to the general air of anticipation, she couldn't tell.

A reporter snapped photos and took details, but at last Tamzin made it to the door, now open invitingly.

She fetched up behind Pen Inkersoll and her family, then murmured, "I love your ink." She wanted to kick herself as Pen turned a startled face.

"Your ink work, I mean," Tamzin corrected, trying not to stare at Pen's dress, which was a sumptuous creation of indigo and gold that would have looked at home at a court ball.

"Thank you! It's a comparatively recent skill. My first husband and I used to work as a team, and he always did the inks. Duffy isn't artistic."

"Oh?" her husband said, switching his dark blue gaze to Pen. "That's not what you said last—"

Pen laughed. "Got you."

"You'll keep, Pen."

Pen turned back to Tamzin. "Bloody fairies. Oops—but I bet you know what I mean." She nodded to Matin. "Elf?" she hazarded.

"Yes," Tamzin said. "Your husband?"

"God knows. Even he doesn't."

They realised Dan Fanshaw was waiting to greet them and turned guilty faces his way.

He gave them a sardonic smile. "Tamzin. Pen. I see you've found a few things in common already."

"With you, too," Pen muttered. "We should start a club—HALF—Human Artists Loving Fairies. How's Nan? I mean, *where's* Nan?"

"Wrangling children when I saw her last. On her way now, I trust. Go on through. Once we're all here, the public can come in."

"God help us then," Pen said.

The gallery was lit with a diffused glow, and Tamzin saw that spotlights had been mounted to illuminate each of the twenty exhibits. All the slots were now occupied, swathed in their white curtains. She found *An Eye for an I,* with the chalk board replaced by an official-looking painted board proclaiming title, artist, and medium.

"This is excruciating," a young woman said, hugging herself. She was dressed in bright red, and not much of it, and with her towering heels, she was taller than almost everyone else in the room.

An older woman, white haired and attractive and draped in a wonderfully detailed embroidered shawl, stood arm in arm with a middle-aged woman in green. "Get me a drop of something strong, will you Marianna?" she said, indicating the refreshment table at the far end of the room.

"Really, Ma?"

"You bet. If Peter were here, he'd be glowering at me, but as he's not . . . quick, before the men come in and start disapproving. A Tom Cat Hill single malt if they have it."

The woman, who had her hair up in a milkmaid braid that reminded Tamzin of her jeweller acquaintance Aureate Shale, headed for the table. When she returned, holding a cut-glass whisky tumbler, Tamzin saw she wore an exhibitor's badge stating her name as Marianna Mackenzie.

More exhibitors and their close associates arrived. Apart from Pen Inkersoll, Tamzin knew none of them by sight until a man with dark red hair and an unassuming air came in. He stood relaxed just inside the door, with his hands in the pockets of well-worn jeans paired with a green and blue plaid shirt.

I know him! The thought was shocking, because although she recognised his face and his stance, she had never associated him with paint, unless it was applied to a fence.

She nudged Matin. "See that red-haired man?"

"Yes."

"I know him!"

"One of your posy of swains?"

"No."

"Is he likely to know you? Under one of your other names, I mean? If so, who will he think you are?"

They'd known it might happen sooner or later.

Tamzin said, "If he does recognise me, which isn't likely, he'll see me as Tamzin Herrick in her first iteration. He was — possibly still is — the groundsman at Diversity High where I went to school for a while."

"Do you want to say hello and take the initiative?"

"I don't know. Maybe. After all, he'll hear and see my name, although he might not remember it."

"Come on, then." Matin, with Fou trundling beside him, took her arm and led her towards the door just as the man, possibly perceiving he was holding up traffic, moved farther in.

They changed direction to intercept him, and he gave them a quizzical, questioning look that changed to doubt, and to uncertain recognition. He glanced at Matin, then back at Tamzin.

Tamzin took the initiative, as Matin had suggested. "Hello, Mister Miller."

He smiled. "Ah, hello. Let me guess . . . Diversity High?"

"Yes! How did you know?"

He held out his left hand and waggled it, displaying a clear ring that appeared to contain a lock of red hair. "I don't get out much, so mostly when someone young and beautiful addresses me, it's because she — or he — remembers me from there." He dropped his gaze to her name badge. "Tamzin Herrick. I do remember you. You used to be fond of that lad with the Chinese puppy."

"Chinese *puppy*?"

He looked guilty. "Forget I said that. It wasn't meant to be unkind. I just recall he often had this small youngster in tow, and he treated her like a little sister — or a pet. She always reminded me of a terrier at that stage. She grew out of it and turned into a charming young woman."

"Lucy Tan," Tamzin said. She laughed. "She's still small, but formidable. She's his cousin."

"You're in touch with the boy then?" Again, his gaze flicked to Matin.

"No. Nor with Lucy. I just happened to see them both a couple of years ago, when I moved back to Sydney. They didn't notice me, and at the time I didn't want to get into the whole *long time no see* thing. This is Matin Campania, my fiancé."

Miller held out his hand. "Good to meet you, Matin. Jack Miller. Mostly, anyway. Today I'm masquerading as —" He tapped his name badge, frowned, and pulled it free of a fold of shirt.

"Jonathan Blarney!" Tamzin exclaimed. "You're *Jonathan Blarney*?"

"Sometimes." He grinned at her. "And I might as well come clean. I was hoping to run across you here, Miss Herrick, to say how much I liked your entry in the Jonathan Blarney Award." He glanced at Matin. "Baby portraits are fiendishly difficult, because babies are either sweet but shapeless or active little tykes with quicksilver in their veins. You have to be quick to sketch that sort. My son was one of them, swimming underwater before he could even toddle. Lucky his mum could keep up with him. I hadn't a hope. Let's see, your subject was called Dickon. Is he yours?"

"No, he belongs to Matin's sister and her husband."

"Then they are to be felicitated."

"Misty and Lars would agree with you," Matin said.

"Fee — my wife — says the secret of good-looking babies is to choose a good man and to make him happy in his contribution." He coughed. "That's not quite what she said, but it's what she meant. I'm well flattered, since Fee could have chosen just about any man alive, and still picked me. I've never been able to find out why."

Tamzin said, "I'll remember that advice."

"Looks to me as if you've made *your* choice already."

"I have. I see you're exhibiting here today."

Miller gave her an impish smile. "I am. Not often illustrators get picked for these things. I reckon they must have an ulterior motive — probably to get as many disciplines as they can while staying in the broad bounds of *picture* rather than moving into sculpture or installation."

"Oh?"

"Gallery Joyce is given over to sculptures, Gallery Mackellar to cloth art and Gallery Spenser to installation. All very hush-hush, is Gallery Spenser. I suspect they're growing glow-in-the-dark mushrooms or something."

Tamzin felt uninformed, but then Miller added, "I didn't know any of that until I got into the website. I had a peep at Joyce and Mackellar, but Spenser isn't open yet, apparently — talk about Area Fifty-One coupled with Fort Knox . . . radioactive alien gold mushrooms . . ." He caught Tamzin's eye and grinned. "Oops, my inner comic book is showing. As I was saying, there are at least two of us who are illustrators — me and Pen Inkersoll. Could be more. I take it you're not an illustrator?"

"Portraitist, mostly," Tamzin said.

"Ah. And our host — or Em-Cee — is a modern *avant-garde* specialist. Missus Mackenzie, there, does future painting, and don't ask me the ins and outs of that. I would like to know how they chose who to invite, but I doubt they'll tell us."

"Who is *they*?" Tamzin asked. She thought Dan Fanshaw, her contact, seemed open and approachable.

"The people behind this complex. Dan's the front man, but he doesn't know any more than we do. It's funded from a grant, or an endowment, dating back — hello, I think something's happening."

He turned his attention to where Dan Fanshaw was tapping on a microphone.

"Good evening, fellow visionaries. I have just a few things to run through for you before we let the public in for the unveiling. You each have a number from one to twenty. Someone will draw numbers out of a hat, and when your number comes up, our audience can gather round and you can then, with as much or as little ceremony as you like, verify that your thumb-printed seal is intact. When that's done, remove the cover from your work. Just drop it on the ground under your piece. It will be collected later. Okay?"

The very tall woman in red said, "What happens then?"

"You should probably stand back a bit so people can see. Don't worry, there won't be a stampede. Only ticket holders can come in tonight, and the numbers are restricted to sixty, excluding your own private plus-ones. We expect to have the reveals made quite quickly. The viewers can look around again at their leisure, probably with a glass of something and a handful of walnuts and cheese."

"Peanuts or lollies," said someone from behind Tamzin.

"No peanuts, because of allergies," Dan said. He went on, "The exhibition is open for at least six months, so anyone who missed out on a ticket can come in at their leisure. We will be recording your reveals—and yes, you will get a chance to vet the recording and have a do-over tomorrow if you feel it necessary—so later patrons can enjoy the moment either on their phones or via larger screens.

"You can stay near your piece to answer any questions, or if you want your work to speak for itself, you can mingle and make like Mona Lisa. Since this is such a personal exhibition, your presentation of yourself forms a part of it. All right?"

"Lot of claptrap if you ask me," the white-haired woman in the embroidered shawl commented.

"Then it's fortunate no one did, Magda." Dan glanced around. "For anyone who hasn't had the pleasure, this is Magda Quest Saxer from *Magdala Gallery* in Western Australia, who acted as agent for some of the most iconic artists' models back in the day — and still does, for that matter. I hope you're not planning to savage anyone this evening, Magda. And I see you haven't brought Peter, for which I am grateful."

She held up the whisky tumbler in ironic salute. "Don't show gratitude too soon, Dan. You never know, with Peter P. He might yet grace us with his presence."

Dan winced perceptibly.

Then he glanced at the screen in front of him. "We're ready to go. Let the great unveiling begin!"

Tamzin looked wonderingly at Jack Miller, who smiled. "This could either be a lot of fun or the biggest debacle ever. Let's stand together for moral support."

"Is your wife here?" Tamzin asked.

Jack's smile never wavered. "That's not possible. Fee doesn't ever come to these events. Neither does our son — Paris. I'll tell them all about it, though."

Tamzin didn't know what to say to that, so she turned to watch the fortunate ticket holders coming in.

The man she'd dubbed Mister Hibiscus, now wearing another loud shirt printed with purple palm trees, was checking electronic tickets and handing out programs as people entered, flowed through, and spread out across the room.

Tamzin saw some bemused glances at the swathed artworks, then the patrons tended to make a comment to their neighbours, or else look down at the program, which, Jack Miller informed her, explained what they'd just been told, as well as some of what he'd found on the website.

Dan waited until everyone was settled before he explained that he'd been asked to Emcee but that, as he was one of the exhibitors, he had withheld his number from the hat so he could go last.

Someone passed him a black top hat, and he pulled out a numbered tile. "We're starting with number fifteen, *Eyes of Day*, by Jonathan Blarney. Jonathan is best known for his watercolour illustrations of his own books—the Bitternut series. He's also the founder of the Jonathan Blarney Award." He paused, evidently waiting.

"That's me then," Jack Miller said. He strolled over to his artwork. "You got that recorder going, Dan?"

Dan Fanshaw nodded and held up a thumb, before glancing down at his screen. "Go ahead."

"Okay. I'm Jonathan Blarney. Years ago, I painted a tea set with waterlilies for my wife, Fee. She's not the acquisitive type, but she's kept that set all this time, and she uses it, too. I still sometimes take her flowers. She likes pink hawthorn, and daisies and roses . . . almost anything as long as it's bright. A big anniversary is coming up for us next year, so I painted her this so she can have flowers even when I haven't had a chance to take her any." He pried up the wax seal and pulled down the covering.

There was a collective murmur as an enormous dished platter emerged. It was made of glazed porcelain and painted with a riot of daisies of every variety Tamzin had seen and several she hadn't.

Jack said, meditatively, "It made a change from illustrating and painting cups and saucers for V-S Roses."

V-S Roses! Yet another link clicked in Tamzin's colliding worlds. Dequan Qin had given her a rose from V-S Roses at their formal, and its name had led, indirectly, to her choice of an alias *and* to the name of her business. Now it seemed Jack Miller was somehow involved in that . . .

She gazed at the platter. It was huge, but also delicate. She moved closer, and spotted, down on the rim, a shamrock leaf, which she recognised as the logo she'd seen on the book series she'd studied in Visual Arts.

Which was taught by Mister Herron, who had a wall of painted china cups and mugs . . .

Jack strolled back and said to Matin, "Not sure that's what they had in mind when they invited me but—" he shrugged. "They *did* say to make it personal."

Matin said, "That's the biggest plate I've ever seen."

"Mad, isn't it?" Jack chuckled. "I wouldn't put it past Fee to serve herself up on that, curled like Cleopatra in a rug."

Dan Fanshaw dipped his hand in the hat again. "Next up— number two—*Aye-Aye and the Giraffe*—collage by Danya Quick."

The tall girl in red said, "Cer-rikey," apologised, and walked over to her piece. She removed the cover and stood back to show a comical, knock-kneed giraffe with a lemur-like creature perched on its head, extending a long middle finger. "That's me," she said, jerking her thumb at the duo.

Someone laughed, choked, and got thumped on the back.

"'Sokay. It's meant to be funny," the artist said.

When the reveals had been made, Tamzin reflected that there was just one thing to say—that the interpretations of the theme were all wildly different.

Her own *Eye for an I* was well received, and she felt rewarded when she saw Matin's appreciative gaze rest on the dolphin pendant she had painted with loving attention. She said little about her inspiration, merely commenting that she, like many other people, had lived as several selves, all of whom integrated in her current one.

She took charge of Fou while Matin went to fetch them drinks from the long table, and since the dog had been so well-behaved, she picked him up to give him praise and a better view than he'd get down by her ankles.

"Won't he wreck your lovely dress?" Pen Inkersoll asked, emerging from the crowd in a flurry of indigo and gold. "I've heard pekes shed like the very dickens."

Tamzin laughed. "Not a chance." She dropped her voice. "Nothing ever happens to this dress—it's fay. You could throw in in a compost heap, cover it and leave it for a month and it would still look like this. I've had it for over a decade."

"Oh. Mine's like that, too." Pen patted her skirts. "A dear friend made this for me when I was feeling sad and dowdy. I don't often get an excuse to wear it, which is one reason I was glad to be invited here. It's spill proof and even cat-proof, which is just as well."

"It's glorious," Tamzin said. She added, "I'm glad you did a magic cat picture for your entry."

Pen looked amused. "I didn't intend to. I was going to do something clever and self-referential, but as soon as I started drawing, *he* showed up and insisted on his place in the sun. *After all . . . I'm the reason you were invited . . .* That's what he said, or implied."

"He?"

"The Cat. Ink Himself." She shrugged. "He's been pushing my artistic buttons off and on for years. I can't complain. I was just about getting by on commissioned illustration after my first husband died, when I gave myself permission to draw Ink for my own enjoyment. The result was *The Magic Cat.* It's been very good to me."

Her husband claimed her attention then, and Tamzin turned to see if Matin was returning. Instead, she came face to face with a red-eyed Emily Scarborough.

"Emily! I didn't know you were coming."

"I didn't tell you, because I wasn't sure if I'd make the cut in the ticket lottery." Emily pushed back her hair. "I wanted to see your painting reveal in person."

Tamzin waited.

"I heard what you told me, about being all those people, about what your parents did, but until I saw your painting, I didn't *understand.* Now I do. I looked at it just now and I *cried."*

"Oh, Emily." Tamzin put her hand out to touch her old friend's arm. She added, "I bought three of your books from *Oranges and Lemons*. It's under new management, but the name's the same."

Emily pursed her lips and put back her hair. "Peter and Jonquil sold out a few years ago, which is disappointing. I don't know why — one day they were there, and when I went there a week or so later the shop was *under new management*." She sighed. "They used to give me personalised displays. I can't get my head around the new owner. He might just as well be selling . . . I don't know . . . packets of barley sugar. He couldn't be less interested — he didn't even bother to change the name of the shop."

"I got that impression, too, but he did have three of your titles, the first two and another one that seems to be the fifth one. I enjoyed them all, and I could hear your voice from years ago. Some of the turns of phrase, and the situations sent me right back there."

Emily's mouth tilted up in a small smile. "Yes, well, we all use the material available to us."

Tamzin added, "And when I read the dedication in *The Red Code,* I was the one crying."

Emily reached out to stroke Fou, and she deftly deflected the subject. "I never knew you were a dog person. I thought it was ponies, ponies, all the way."

"I like dogs, though I've never had one. Fou isn't mine. I'm looking after him for someone else."

"He's so well behaved," Emily said.

"Yes. He's an odd little being."

Emily pushed her hair back again. "Tamzin, where do we go from here?"

"I don't know. We live in different states, so we can't exactly go riding together every Monday or drop by for coffee."

Unless I get Matin to send me through the gate . . . but how do I explain that?

"No. I have Jamie and the girls, and you have your fiancé. Pop approved of him, by the way. That's more of a compliment than you know. Pop doesn't make a habit of voicing approval."

"So I gathered. He certainly didn't approve of Mister Sinister."

"Who?"

"That's my private name for my presumed, peculiar, and peripatetic father."

"And your mother is Missus Sinister?"

Tamzin laughed. "No. Are you analysing me?"

"Would I?"

"Maybe. I don't know. Anyhow, my mother is Ada. I have no idea why." She paused for a few seconds and made an unpremeditated suggestion. "Emily, if you wanted, we could do a project together, just for fun. I know your publisher probably picks your illustrators, but if you wanted to write a different story —"

"You'd do the illustrations?"

"It's just an idea. You could send me the instalments, the way we used to work, only long distance."

Emily said, "Mostly if people make offers like that, I have to turn them down as tactfully as I can. But your stuff is pro-level. And I've always wanted to write a fantasy adventure, you know, set in another world. I keep seeing a gorgeous place coloured with that soft blue-purple jacarandas have. My publisher wants more of the series I'm doing now, because that's where the market is, but if I come up with a story line . . . maybe?"

"Yes. If you like, send it to me. You have my email address."

"We could try a boutique publisher, or even self-publish . . . wouldn't be very profitable, but there has to be more to life than profit. There has to be . . . magic."

Tamzin looked at her oldest friend and felt a surge of fel-low-feeling.

I've found my magic – I've lived it every day since Rochelle ran away.

She said, "By the way, have you ever written song lyrics?"

Emily bit her lip. "I write verse, but I don't play any instruments."

"I do." She realised Matin had come up behind her, and she set Fou down so she could take her drink.

"Hello again, Tamzin's fiancé," Emily said.

"Hello, Tamzin's oldest friend. Can I get you anything?" Matin said.

"No, thanks. I already had a glass of something purple and scary. The server said it was a Jacaranda Haze. I have to get going, but it was lovely to catch up again. And Tamzin, I'll think about what you said and be in touch. I mean that."

Emily held out her hand to each of them in turn, turned and walked away.

Matin gazed after her. "All right, my dolphin?"

"Fine. We were just laying some ghosts, and maybe some pavers in a pathway."

"Speaking of *laying*," he said.

"Yes, please."

Tamzin finished her drink and went to find Dan Fanshaw to take her leave before she followed Matin and Fou outside.

They elected to walk around the gallery complex in the op-posite direction to avoid the crowd of people heading for ve-hicles. The other small galleries had lit-up signs, and Tamzin paused to read the names and dates of current and upcoming exhibitions, including Light and Line Sculpture and The Set-tlers' Path Quilting. Then they were approaching the entrance to the big main gallery, which Jack Miller had considered a cross between Area Fifty-One and Fort Knox.

Gallery Spenser – Project Twenty-Five, opening March first.

"That's my birthday," Tamzin remarked. She thought back

to the birthday that had brought her to tears and to happiness in Matin's arms.

I won't have to cry this year. I can go straight to the happiness.

Matin said, "Shall we come and have a look at that to celebrate?"

"I don't know — I mean, Mister Miller said it was installation, and that means it could be anything!"

"Glow in the dark radioactive alien mushrooms," Matin recalled.

"And it's only a few weeks away —"

"It doesn't take long to get here," he reminded.

"That's very true." She recalled her conflicted thoughts about how possible and even easy it would have been to visit Emily every week — and how impossible it would have been to explain.

A sliver of light gleamed from the blacked-out windows of Gallery Spenser, and Matin paused, listening.

Tamzin couldn't hear anything, but she knew he had much sharper hearing than hers. "What is it? Radioactive aliens?"

"Someone talking inside. Arguing, really."

"I expect —" Tamzin broke off with a yelp as Fou, who had been sauntering along on a slack leash, reared back, raised his blunt little face skywards and slipped his collar. Before Tamzin could react, he'd taken off at the closest thing he had to a gallop, straight to the door of Gallery Spenser.

Chapter Thirteen: The Bear

Tamzin Herrick, February, 2020

Fou scrabbled madly at the door of Gallery Spenser with his front paws, behaving more like a hyperactive terrier than his usual laidback Pekingese self.

If he'd yelped or whined, it might have seemed more ordinary, but, apart from the sound of claws on metal, he was silent.

Tamzin stared at him, frozen in place. "Matin—"

Her betrothed's hand closed comfortingly on her arm. "Try calling him."

"He won't hear." But she tried anyway. "Fou! Come on. Belly rubs!"

Fou continued to rip at the door.

"He's going to hurt himself." Tamzin approached her charge and attempted to lift him away from the door.

He jack-knifed in her hands, scratching her inadvertently. It was like trying to hold a large, muscular fish, and the thick, slippery fur made it impossible to keep her grip. To her shame, Tamzin let go.

Fou hit the ground, scrambled up, and dived for the door again. He went back to trying to dig his way through solid steel.

"Matin?"

He was by her side in a second. "What do you want me to do?"

The words could have sounded impatient or querulous,

but his tone was warm.

"We could get his collar back on." She undid the empty collar and looped it around the dog's neck, buckling it into the keeper.

She tugged the leash, and Fou came away from the door, but he spelled reluctance in every protesting movement. His braced paws slid on the pavement.

"What does he *want*?"

"To get in there," Matin said.

That was obvious, she supposed.

Tamzin pushed at the door. She tried the handle, but it was all too obviously locked from the inside. She couldn't even rattle it, and a knock made embarrassingly little sound.

"There might be something wrong—thieves, or vandals," she ventured, though why that should concern Fou she didn't know. "Or fire." But again, why would Fou care?

"Or a plague of rats," Matin said dryly. She looked up and he grimaced. "Do pekes hunt rats?"

"That's a terrier thing, but I suppose he might—you said someone was arguing. What about?"

"I don't know. I tuned it out."

Tamzin relaxed her tension on the leash and Fou flew back at the door. "If I asked you to open that door, what would you say?"

"I'd point out that it's a grey area. I have no right to open that door, since it's locked. It doesn't belong to me, and I have no reason to believe anyone inside needs my help."

Tamzin waited, sensing a *but*.

It soon came. "On the other hand, I see leaving it closed is causing distress to the emperor, and by extension to my be-loved, for whom I would do *anything*. Therefore, I'll try to conjure it open. I can't swear it will work."

Tamzin gave him a grateful look. She understood this was on the edge of what Matin would be able to do. Conjuring depended upon the object being something the protagonist could achieve, physically and ethically, by other means. Like *going*, which allowed fay to bypass the tyranny of distance *over there*, conjuring allowed them to bypass inconveniences such as finding a magnet and a string to fish a pin out of a drain. Matin could undoubtedly hire a bulldozer to get that door open, or find someone with a master key, so the rub lay in the ethical clause.

She crossed her fingers and wished hard that the desires of a small and hairy despot and her obligation to keep her lodger safe would outweigh any consideration of the gallery owners' right to keep their door locked.

He's middle-aged. He's a peke. He could have a heart attack.

Of course, she could scoop him up and carry him away, but he might still be distressed.

"It's open," Matin said quietly.

Now what?

"I don't think we can let him go in alone. We'll go with him." He conjured a torch, which Tamzin recognised as being one he usually kept at his flat.

Tamzin reflected that breaking and entering with an elf didn't actually include the *breaking* bit, since nothing was forced or broken. She half-expected someone to yell out to know what they were doing, but they stepped in unmolested.

She had previously seen light through the edge of the window, but when they stepped inside, all was dark.

Fou dragged at his leash determinedly, but Matin closed the door behind them and murmured, "Wait."

They waited.

Tamzin's eyes adjusted, and she saw dark shapes emerging from the flat blackness. A faint glow resolved into a clock-face with a new moon, hanging far above eye level.

Her fingers closed hard on Matin's as something tweaked her memory.

Nightlight. Love you over the moon.

"I think we need the torch," Matin said in the same low tone.

"Yes. No radioactive glowing alien mushrooms."

"Not so far." He switched it on, and soft, diffused light brought a view of partitions with doors and a spiral staircase leading up to a mezzanine level.

Tamzin looked about and saw the partitions bore cards, pencilled with names and dates.

She opened a door at random.

Bryn and Angharad Thomas, Jingleup, WA, July 2015. Kitchen.

"Could these be storage units?" she asked, puzzled.

Fou whined and pulled the leash.

"It looks more like a working kitchen," Matin said.

Tamzin saw he was right. Nothing was packed away or covered in dust sheets. A newspaper rested on a round table with a cloth embroidered with a red Welsh dragon.

A book lay face-down by the paper. Tamzin squinted to read the title. *Cymru Abroad, B.A. Thomas.*

Two coffee cups, which were also dragon-patterned, stood upside down on the draining board by the sink, alongside a ceramic pot holding a washing-up brush and some steel wool.

A laptop bag sat near the door, and a coat was flung over one of the kitchen chairs.

Tamzin, towing the reluctant Fou, moved to the refrigerator. It was stocked with long-life milk, eggs and some labelled containers.

The cupboards revealed thick white crockery, measuring jugs, a grater, a blender, and an assortment of packets and cans. Tamzin lifted down a packet of tea. It was still in its plastic wrapper, but when she turned it over, the *best before* date read July, 2016. A dozen receipts in a brass bowl revealed that groceries had been bought for cash at Jingleup Fresh on dates ranging throughout June and July 2015. The latest was dated July 17th. A receipted bill for electricity in the name of B. Thomas lay with an unopened bank statement. A bowl with a half-empty bag of toffees, two champagne corks, some rubber bands, and a hair clip sat on top of the fridge. A calendar for 2015 sported pictures of Wales. It was open at July. Three dates were ringed and annotated, but Tamzin couldn't read the words in the poor light. She picked up a pair of glasses and squinted through them. They appeared to be plain magnifiers.

"What on earth?" she said.

Matin peered at the calendar. "Bryn had to buy a card for someone called Ellie, and someone — possibly Angharad — had a hair appointment with CC." He flipped back through the calendar. "More of the same."

"It looks like the Mary Celeste!" Tamzin said. She glanced at Matin to see if he understood the reference. She had missed a good deal of human culture during her late teens and early twenties, but Matin had spent most of his childhood *over there,* and so he couldn't be expected to be quite as immersed in history and folklore as a human.

He nodded. "No half-eaten meals, though. What did your red-haired friend say this place was used for?"

"Mister Miller? He's not exactly a friend. He was the groundsman at school. Oh — wait. He said this was going to house installations."

"Which are? Alien mushrooms?"

"He was joking. It's an art term. Life-size pieces that are three-dimensional and arranged to look like something functional. More or less."

"Then *this* is an installation of a room belonging to people called Bryn and Angharad Thomas," he said.

"Oh. Of course! The date and place stamping! It's a kind of character sketch of a couple's kitchen, like those historic houses that are kept exactly as they were when someone famous lived there."

"Oh?"

"Yes, I heard of one where an early female politician lived. Her knitting and the newspaper she was reading before she died are still there on the coffee table. I expect someone dusts them . . . But look, there are clues all over. One of these people at least wore reading glasses, and they lived in a small town. They were either Welsh immigrants or else they were descended from Welsh people. They probably wrote this book —" Tamzin picked it up and looked at the back cover. It showed two people, holding up a map of Wales superimposed on a map of Australia. Their faces were obscured by the map, but one wore a shirt depicting an Australian flag, and the other had the Welsh dragon.

"Shoes." Matin pointed out a pair of hiking boots on one of the chairs. A park guide was stuck inside one of them.

"This is so bizarre." Tamzin tugged at Fou's leash. It came forward without restriction. She froze.

Matin glanced down. "Where's the emperor?"

"He's slipped his collar. Again."

"He must be in here somewhere," Matin said reasonably. Typically, he said nothing about her carelessness in not tightening the collar.

"Of course. You closed the door, so he's in here somewhere . . ."

The trouble with looking for a dog in a dark gallery full of different rooms was that they couldn't rely on him to stay put. It wasn't like looking for a pair of socks.

Tamzin called Fou softly, but she knew he wouldn't come.

The upside was that the doors to each installation were closed, and not even Fou could phase through solid timber.

Tamzin suddenly remembered the schemers, fay cats that had lived in the stable house when she stayed with Andy on Summer Island. She suspected *they* could phase.

"Matin, Fou's not a fay dog, is he?"

"Not as far as I know. I've never seen a peke living *over*

there."

So he really can't phase. Nevertheless, Tamzin opened the next door from pure curiosity.

The label stated that this one was a bedroom belonging to Tim and Amy Keats, *ACT, September 2017.*

The torchlight darted about, spotlighting the room's features. A queen-sized bed bore a quilt straight out of a mail-order catalogue, where it would have been advertised as *pure cream elegance with a sophisticated touch of coffee.* The sheets were also coffee, and the bedroom suite was a matched set of walnut veneer. A water glass sat on one bedside table, and one lamp had a mis-matched globe. A pair of electric blue slippers had trodden-down heels. The pictures on the wall featured white horses with wind-tossed manes in frames edged with old gold. A brown velvet cushion on the bed had vintage costume jewellery pinned to it. An untidy pile of home improvement magazines sported yellow sticky notes. An unwritten postcard showing the Canberra War Memorial was stuck haphazardly in the mirror frame.

"Fou?"

"He's not here," Matin said, shifting the light from a tangle of odd socks in a box by the wardrobe and a basket of wool with knitting needles stuck in a coffee-coloured skein.

"But who are these people?" Tamzin asked. "I mean, are they real, do you think? Or are they made up?"

Matin shook his head. He pulled out the drawer in the foot of the bed, which proved to be full of summer clothing. He unfolded a khaki fishing jacket with an inkstain on the pocket.

Under the clothes, the drawer was lined with newspaper, dated December 2016.

"It looks real," he said.

"How do you mean?"

Matin held out a sheet of the lining paper. "If this had been set up, surely they would have used a paper from September

2017."

Tamzin thought back. "I suppose so. Whereas anyone who really lined their drawers like this would leave it in place until it got — well, forever, I guess, until they moved or got a new suite."

Matin turned, sweeping the light with him. "Did you hear that?"

"No."

"I think it's the emperor. Come on." He replaced the paper and clothing and closed the drawer.

The next room was different, having a small frame cut in the bottom of the door. The space was filled with a swinging flap.

"That's a dog door!" Tamzin said.

Matin opened the door and stuck his head in. "He's here."

This room was what Tamzin thought might have been termed a boot room or a laundry. Raincoats hung from hooks on the wall, and there was a metal sink, too big for dishes. A watering can and some garden tools occupied floor to ceiling shelves, and by an old refrigerator was a well-used dog bed, with a leash hanging above it.

In the bed Fou lounged, and he wasn't alone. He had one paw on a disreputable teddy bear.

"Fou!" Tamzin said.

He looked up at her and flipped his tail a couple of times.

"I suppose this is why he wanted to come in here," Matin said.

"What, to go to bed? But that's —"

"Bizarre? Not if it's his own bed. And, assuming that toy is also his . . ."

Tamzin said, "Nell Andover's Pepe has a toy Nell calls his stuffie. He has it in the sling when she carries him, and it goes in the van with him. He'll settle anywhere if he has his stuffie. It always comes along to festivals, and when she washes it, he sits under the line until it's dry." She added plaintively, "But how can these things be Fou's? His bed is back in Fiddler's Rest."

Matin moved to the door to shine the light on the label.

Clemency and Aubree Barrett, Parson Bay, NSW, December 2019. Fou's Mud Room.

Tamzin stared uncomprehendingly from the label back at Fou. She looked at the leash and collar she had in her hand and compared it with the one hanging above the dog bed. They were identical, except that the one she had was newer.

There were identical brushes, too, one with a tuft of hair that matched the peke's. An almost full bag of kibble stood by the fridge with the top neatly tucked over.

"Clem and Breezy," Tamzin said. She unhooked one of the raincoats. Beside it hung a familiar-looking cape. "Why?"

Matin said, "This is strange . . . but we've solved Fou's mystery. He obviously detected his own things in here, and maybe he thought he smelled his owners."

"Do you think this is where they went when they left him with me? If they came here to help set up the installations for the gallery, maybe they thought they wouldn't have time to look after him."

"They obviously didn't bargain for you being invited to exhibit in the same complex and bringing Fou with you," Matin said.

"Maybe we wouldn't have brought him if we hadn't been able to come through the gates. But what now? If Breezy is *here*, do I take Fou home or leave him with her? And *where* is she? A hotel? Staying with friends? Renting?"

Matin had no immediate answer to that, and Tamzin didn't blame him. She had begun to develop a headache, and she thought the best thing was probably to go back to the *Harvest Hob* with Fou and return the next day to try to find his owners.

As for the peculiarity of finding people she knew, though only slightly, featuring as characters in an installation, she supposed that was yet another clashing of her worlds.

She put the collar on Fou, tightening it this time to prevent him from slipping it again. He obviously didn't want to leave what must be familiar to him, and so, with considerable reluctance, she picked up the battered toy and tucked it under her arm.

It's not theft, she assured herself. *It obviously belongs to Fou.*

The dog followed willingly, and Tamzin was about to ask Matin to let them out when a thought struck her. The three rooms they'd entered had all been apparently modelled on houses belonging to different people in different years and in different places. The fact that she knew two of the people was odd, but—

A door closed overhead.

We ought to leave.

Fear crushed her so suddenly, she reeled. "Matin, can we go? Now?"

"If you want," he said.

Tamzin bent and scooped Fou into her arms, bundling him together with his toy. She hurried after Matin as if being pursued by a nightmare.

CHAPTER FOURTEEN: FLITTED

Tamzin Herrick, February, 2020

Tamzin's twenty-eighth birthday fell three weeks after their return from Adelaide.

The week before it, little had changed. Fou was still with her, and she had still had no word from Breezy and Clem.

She now knew their full names, but they remained enigmas otherwise. They shared a surname, but they clearly weren't sisters or mother and daughter. They looked nothing alike, despite the way they dressed, and they had different accents. They really were a couple, she supposed, either married or using the same surname for convenience.

She had asked Dan Fanshaw about them before leaving Adelaide, but he said he knew no one of those names or descriptions. He said he would ask Wayne, but he didn't say when. Since she couldn't admit to breaking into Gallery Spenser, Tamzin had to drop it.

We should have gone upstairs when we heard the door close.

Once back at Fiddler's Rest, she enquired among the Dames for anyone with contact details for Breezy and Clem. It was a reasonable thing to do, considering she had temporary custody of their dog.

The Dame network was effective, as usual, and Florida Klim, who rode a motorcycle with her border collie, Harley, on the pillion during her infrequent get-togethers with the others at the dog park, obligingly dug through her phone records to find a call from Breezy Barrett.

"Lucky I never remember to delete my phone history," she said, scrolling cheerfully. "Mind, I'd better get on to it, or I'll run out of space. Here—got it. At least, I think so. It's from last year." She handed Tamzin the phone. "Call her on this, if you like."

Tamzin could think of no valid reason not to call in front of Florida, so she hit the contact and raised the phone to her ear.

For a moment she thought Breezy had answered, but then she realised it was a mechanical voice. *The mobile you are trying to call . . .*

She listened to full message, pressed *end* and handed the phone back to Florida.

"No luck?"

"It says the phone is disconnected," she said.

"Looks to me as if you've got yourself a dog," Florida responded. She patted Harley. Watch out Elfie . . . incoming!"

Tamzin bent to pick up a rolling ball and tossed it back into a crowd of gleeful terriers.

Lise Pomfrey, one of the younger terrier Dames, raised a cheerful thumb in response.

Tamzin grinned at her and turned her attention back to Florida. "They can't have vanished off the—" She broke off, for hadn't *she* effectively vanished for seven years? Anyone seeking her in that time would have drawn a blank unless he or she happened to interview Otto Fairling.

"No, but there has to be a statute of limitations," Florida said, scratching Harley behind the ear. "For example, my niece got a pup when she was sixteen. Present from her boyfriend. They split a few months later. After a couple more years, she went off to university, and left Maxi with her mum and dad. For a while she talked about finding a place where she could have Maxi with her, but then after a bit she stopped mentioning it. She finished her course and got a job overseas and it just became understood that Maxi was staying with my sister."

"Is she still there?" Tamzin asked.

Florida said gently, "Yes, in the manner of speaking. My sister has a nice little urn with Maxi's name on it. Lived to be fifteen. My niece had been back for five years, and she still hadn't found a place with room for a dog. I did say to my sister that she should send the urn, and the bill, to Maxi's official owner. That wasn't well received."

"Your niece didn't disappear, though?" Tamzin said.

"No. There is that. She'd ask after Maxi whenever she called, and she'd give her lots of loving attention when she came to visit. She sometimes sent toys or bags of snacks through the post. She was even sad when Maxi went off where good dogs go . . . and she was a good little dog." She shrugged. "And who's to say what Maxi would have wanted? She was happy with my sister.

"As for Fou, though — if he stays with you much longer, Breezy might decide it's just easier to leave him with you for good. He's not fretting, is he?"

"No. He's mostly easy-going."

"There you are, then. Sorry she didn't answer her phone."

"It's not your fault."

"I didn't mean that. If she *had* answered, I'd have been inclined to give her an earful. This might be a soft abandonment, but it's still abandonment, and it's damned bad manners. No care packages of snacks have arrived, I assume?"

"Not one. She played me for an idiot," Tamzin said. "I should have asked for contact details and got her to give me a timeline. I should have got her vet's details, too, and an emergency next of kin. I never thought of it. I've never had a dog, so there are probably all sorts of things I don't know."

"She may have chosen you for that reason." Florida looked thoughtfully at Tamzin. "I know where they live, if that's any help. I could take you there."

Tamzin accepted the offer. She and Florida weren't close,

but it was typical of the Dames that one should be so helpful. She wasn't sure about riding on a motorbike, but Florida assured her they could go in Tamzin's van.

"That way Harley and Fou can both come with us," she said. "Want to go now?"

"Now?"

"Why not? Give your fella a call if you want to let him know where you'll be."

"I'm not seeing him today." Tamzin loaded her passengers in the van, and they drove up the coast to Parson Bay. The settlement was quite close to Fiddle Bay, but Tamzin had not had reason to visit it before.

Florida turned out to be an admirable navigator. She didn't remember the names of roads and streets, but she did remember the layout. "They're at the end of one of those roads that heads out of town. The house is set back, so it's not that easy to see. Turn off here. There's a concealed opening sign in about half a k, and it's down in there."

When they reached the address Florida remembered, Tamzin had a moment of déjà vu as she saw a pet door.

She took Fou with her, and he certainly recognised the place. He cocked his leg against a mossy step before he headed for his private door. He pushed it with his paw and looked annoyed when it failed to open. He tried again, barging it with his flat muzzle, but the door was apparently barred.

"Sorry, Fou," Tamzin said as she scooped him up. She knocked at the front door, but she was unsurprised when no one answered.

Taking a chance, she peeped in the window of the room with the dog door.

"Fou's mud room," she confirmed. The room was cleared, but a pale patch showed where the big sink had stood, and she saw a nail where the leash had hung, and pegs that had held the coats and capes.

She found Florida wandering around the garden, carrying a flyer she had taken from the letterbox. "Letter-dropped — no stamp." She held it up. "Not one of mine, though — I drop for a couple of catalogue companies. That's how I knew this was the place . . . Breezy was out in the garden when I came by. She headed over to tell me off for dropping unsolicited mail, recognised me, and gave me a coffee instead. Clem was in the kitchen, but she didn't say much, other than *hiya*."

Tamzin stared at her. "You've got a good memory."

"It's handy for the letterboxing run. I remember who's receptive and who's likely to set the dog on me — so to speak." She chuckled. "This looks pretty conclusive to me," she added, rubbing her hand through her iron-grey curls. "No addressed mail. No tools left out. Lawn dying off. If you look through the kitchen window everything's been cleared. Want to go down to the post office?"

"Might as well, if you direct me."

"Just back to town, and it's in the main street. We can get a snack at the bakery. I always do when I'm on a run."

The post office clerk was uncommunicative, refusing to confirm whether or not Aubree and Clemency Barrett still had a mailing address in the town. In fact, she wouldn't even confirm that they had ever had one. Fortunately, a customer, perhaps tired of standing in line to be served while Tamzin questioned the clerk, was less reticent.

"If you mean those Canadian women with the little dog, they left before Christmas. I know it was then, because Clem used to sing in the church choir, and someone else had to take over her solo at about five minutes' notice."

"Do you have any idea where they went?" Tamzin asked.

"I've got a feeling Clem was going back to the states — or Canada, I suppose. Dunno about Aubree. I did hear they had a bust-up." She shrugged. "There's someone else moving in next week."

Tamzin thanked the talkative woman and went thoughtfully back to the van.

Florida was lounging against it eating a custard tart. "Got one for you if you want it," she said. "The guys got a sausage roll. Not good for them, but a dog's got to have some guilty pleasures." She rolled her eyes sideways at Tamzin. "Speaking of which—I hear your Fou is going to be a daddy."

"What?"

"Daylight Pengellis . . . Daylight Rosebay, I mean. Her Shelley's up the duff, and she says Fou is the man in in the frame." Her amusement deepened. "You didn't know?"

"I knew it was a possibility, but Daylight hasn't said anything to me."

"You didn't hear it from me, then. But I will say they'll probably be nice little beasts. If Daylight is looking for homes, I might get one for my sister." She gave a snort of amusement. "Jackapeke. Sounds like something out of a movie."

"How do you feel about keeping him?" Matin asked when Tamzin reported that Fou's owners had flitted.

"I won't mind, but it would have been nice if they'd been upfront and *told* me they weren't coming back."

"Would you have agreed to take him if you'd known?"

"I don't know. Probably. You know I was open to having a dog if one came into my life. I wouldn't have picked a Pekingese, but he's not much trouble."

Matin said, "He was a deal less trouble before he got his bear back. That thing seems to have a mind of its own. It's always just behind you, waiting for you to trip. Maybe it's secretly a radioactive alien."

"Whatever it is, it needs washing. I'll have to ask Nell about the care and sanitising of soft dog toys. I don't think I ought to boil it the way I do washing-up cloths."

Matin said, "I can fix that."

"Elf dry-cleaning? I love it! You could start a business."

Matin bit his lip and looked away.

"Bleddy hell! You mean you *have*?"

"When I was younger, I saw a human maid crying because she'd dropped red wine on a shirt she shouldn't have been wearing. I—"

"You offered to clean it for her. My hero!"

He shrugged. "I did service a few clients there for a while."

"I'm never going to exhaust your possibilities, am I?"

"I do hope not, my dolphin." He gestured to the studio he was fitting up for her in Delphinium House. "What do you think?"

"I think it's marvellous. When can we move in?"

"Any time now. Do you want to bring your bed from Fiddler's Rest? Or any other furniture?"

"I think we might leave that furnished. I didn't choose what's there—it came with the house."

Matin wrinkled his face. "I'm rather attached to that bed."

"I'm sure we could use the one already here. Or we could have a better one. Maybe springyweed? Or fresh seadown?" She looked at him hopefully.

"Seadown, now—will you ask Mariner van der Strand about that, or shall I broach the lovely Meribelle?"

"You wouldn't dare."

"No, and neither would you. Mariner is too appreciative of your attributes for comfort."

Tamzin grinned. "He is, isn't he? Even though Meri tries to drown him whenever he says so. You'd think he'd learn."

"You can't drown a seaman. They have sea gift, like the fisherfolk."

"That's good to know. We could gather some seadown ourselves next time we go to the Charms."

"We'll do that, then. Want to go now?"

"That's what I love about you . . . you make things happen. I do want to go now, but I have to get back to Fiddler's Rest and finish that commission for Annie Blue. Maybe we can go next week."

He nodded. "Unless you want to bring your own bed here."

Tamzin moved back a step so she could look into his clear hazel eyes. "Matin, what *is* it with you and my bed? It's a bed! It's a good one, and we've had a lot of fun in it, but as I said, I didn't choose it, any more than we chose the one that's here. I do think a new one is the way to go."

Matin looked away.

"Stop being shifty. It isn't like you. Do I have to threaten your cock with an ice pack?"

He winced, and his eyes widened.

"Okay, so you'd enjoy that. And I thought *I* was the kinky one."

He sighed. "I used to be an in-and-out, that-was-lovely man. You're rubbing off on me."

"I should hope so. We've been rubbing against one another for a long time, now. But don't change the subject. Bed."

"Now?"

"Matin! Do I have to tie your cock in a knot?"

"You can always try."

"*Bleddy hell!* Just tell me!"

He shrugged. "If you must have it, I don't want to think of Olivier making Nessa squeal in that bed. That's all."

Tamzin stared at him. "Nessa's said yes to him?"

"I don't know—exactly—but she's wearing her earring again, and she's shortened it. She's rocking some man's world, and I think it's probably Olivier, judging by the dazed look of delight in his eyes."

"Unless she's taken up with the godbrothers."

"I doubt that. I think they're on the hunt for colleens. A

pisky minx would be too impatient with them, and leppys love gold."

"Why didn't you tell me you'd seen them? Olivier and Nessa, I mean."

He said, "They came through on Monday and we had supper. You were busy with that mosaic, and if I'd called you it would have been over an hour before I could get to you to bring you through . . . or down the coast."

"Yes, I know—" She bit her lip. "Matin, we've got to move in together. I'm missing you too much, being still at Fiddler's Rest." She added, "Olivier's going to take it on?"

"We did talk about it."

"Yes—yes, and I think it's a grand idea. Aunt Mim will be glad of the company. I can't think of anyone I'd rather see living there. As for the bed—what if we bring it here, and set it up in that little secret room? We can have a new one, and still go and bounce about in my old one for old time's sake. Olivier can make his own arrangements, and so can Mim."

He kissed her gratefully.

"You only had to say so," she said.

"Where's the fun in that? My reticence got me an offer of an iced cock. I'm officially asking for a raincheck."

"You!" She flung herself down on the couch and they wrestled until they were both laughing.

Tamzin got up reluctantly. "I'd better go and get this job done."

"Yes." He got up too, looking ruefully down at himself. "You're right. We need to be together. I'll come to you when I finish here." He added abruptly, "The Gallery Spenser exhibition is opening on Sunday."

"I know. Dan sent us an invitation."

"Did you accept?"

"I thought—I—"

"Mistress, I think we need to go, if only for Fou's sake. And after all, one of the installations is missing a stuffed bear. It might be politic if we take a new one to replace the one we appropriated."

"You cleaned the old one for me. Can you dirty up a new one, so they don't know the difference?" She sighed. "All right. We'll go. I'll call Sheelagh and see if we can have the same room again."

Chapter Fifteen: Gallery Spenser

Tamzin Herrick, March 1st, 2020

Tamzin considered buying a new dress for the Gallery Spenser opening, but in the end, she decided not to bother. Matin loved her green dress, and she knew it was the most becoming thing she owned, excepting, possibly, her ballgown, and that was a bit too formal for a gallery opening. She wondered briefly if the *Fairings* shop still existed. It should be easy enough to find out. She didn't remember the address, but it would be online. If it had changed hands, a visit might prove disappointing, as her visit to *Oranges and Lemons* had proved, but she would find out.

It crossed her mind she might find something there to wear for her wedding.

For the gallery, though, she was again in her green dress and her spy-heeled shoes with her dolphin pendant and her betrothal ring. She also had a new bracelet that matched the ring . . . a gift from Matin, made by Aureate Shale.

"When did you get this?" she asked, clasping it on and enjoying the dewdrop sparkle.

"Do you remember when I delivered the hands and rings painting you did for Aureate and Jervey in exchange for our betrothal rings? I asked for it then."

"So now we owe them something else."

"No, dear heart. I took them some applewood. Jervey wanted to try his hand at carving wood from *over here,* and he liked your pendant."

"It's perfect. Did you make the kissing dolphin clasp, or did he?"

"I did. I think I'm turning into a pixie."

"I beg your pardon, Master Campania? I can't see any green in your complexion."

"Jealousy. It's my problem, and I won't let it become yours — ever."

She looked at him, puzzled. "I thought elf men were the nicest . . . not jealous like pixies, or manipulative like piskies, or uppity like courtfolk men?"

"You forgot hobs and braefolk, treefolk, leppys . . . but I take your meaning. We work hard at projecting the pleasant image. Jealousy never troubled me until I met you again, but now I find I want to be the one who delights you . . . even if it means taking a tiny share of the thanks from Mistress Shale."

"I see." She touched the clasp of the bracelet.

"Is that all you have to say?"

"No, there are two more things. One is that you *are* the one who delights me in ways no one else ever has or ever will. The other is that I will hold you to your agreement that I am free to spend time with friends and clients, without permission or silent objection from you. However, I want very much for us to spend more time together. I miss you horribly when you're not with me."

He nodded silently.

"So now, with me being in possession of the most beautiful bracelet that will join my other favourite things — what are we going to do about Fou today? Is it fair to take him to the gallery again when it upset his furry little applecart last time?"

"Pity we can't ask him," Matin said.

"I wonder if we could get Lady Velvet to have a word."

To her relief, Matin appeared to give that serious thought. Lady Velvet was Gillan St Ives' mani-self, a dignified and civilised spaniel bitch. She and Fou had spent time together at

Christmas.

Matin said, "We could try, but I don't think it would work. The mani dogs do play with natural dogs—well, you've seen the Black Douglas at the dog park and with Shelley—but I don't think they communicate in our terms. Lady Velvet might understand Fou, but I don't think she could or would ask him a direct question, or that Gillan could interpret her experience when she's in her minx form."

"That's what I thought. I remember Zennor telling me he never knew what Demi-dog looked like until I did a sketch, because Demi isn't interested in mirrors and won't look at them. It would be too easy if muties could find things out from true animals. You'd have muties Doctor Doolittling all over the place."

"It could be awkward if it worked that way," Matin said.

"*Bleddy hell*! Um . . . Matin, if two people with mani selves get together—say the way Zen and Githa have—do *their* dogselves ever have—well—pups together?"

Matin looked as disconcerted as she had ever seen him. "I have no idea! You'd have to ask Githa or Zen. It's a rare manifest, so the chance of a match between two of them is even rarer."

"Maybe they don't know either," Tamzin mused.

"Well—they might be in for a surprise, although Demi-dog is probably a bit too insubstantial and ethereal to plant a litter, even if he had the desire to. But what about Fou? Do you want him to stay with Bran and Gillan or with Mum and Dad?"

"I think we'll take him to the Hob. He'll be pleased to see his kelpie friend again."

Fou got willingly into the van, and having driven to the castle bridge gate, walked to the Cornfellow holdings and returned to the human realm via the scullery at the pub, Tamzin and Matin left their bags in their room and set out for the gallery complex. Fou stayed behind with Sheelagh's dog, whose eyebrows went into overdrive when she saw him again.

Sheelagh said, "I was hoping ye'd bring darlin' Fou along, dearie. Riannan is wantin' his attentions."

Tamzin nodded doubtfully. If Sheelagh meant what she thought she did, then the logistics seemed insurmountable, but she supposed Fou would know. Maybe he could stand on a hassock. She was sure Sheelagh would provide one.

In the tap room, she took Matin's offered arm and accepted two name badges from Master Applebee.

"Ready, Master Campania?"

"Always."

The walk to the gallery complex was familiar, but when they arrived, the crowd was no bigger than before. She had expected a lot more people wanting to see the so-secretive gallery contents.

She whispered, "Are you going to place the toy now?"

"Already done," Matin replied. "As near as possible to the way it looked before."

Tamzin gave a tiny laugh. "We'll feel like idiots if they've already replaced it . . ."

"They can always remove the less authentic one."

"That'll be theirs," she said with satisfaction. The replacement bear had been left in Fou's bed for a few hours to acquire some of his hair and smell. They had experimented with swapping it out for his original one, but Fou had not been fooled. He had vociferously demanded *his* bear.

Tamzin felt a quiver of apprehension run through her. Now they were there, she hoped no one accused them of trespass. What if there had been CCTV cameras in the gallery when they made their sortie before? What if they'd left DNA, fingerprints . . .

Bleddy hell — aside from my bracelet, we're even wearing the same outfits!

She pictured the news report. *Fiddle Bay Artist and Music Producer Boyfriend Caught on Camera . . ."The elves made me do it," Tamzin Herrick claims.*

She drew a deep, shaky breath.

Matin squeezed her hand. "It will be all right."

"I'm glad you think so."

She looked for friendly faces . . . Dan, Pen, Emily, Danya, or even Jack Miller or Magda and her daughter, but most of them would have no reason to be here today. Even Dan was a no-show. Presumably, he was babysitting the 2020 Vision exhibition, which still had some months left to run.

She spotted the man she'd dubbed Mister Hibiscus, checking tickets in a booth by the door Matin had conjured open on their previous visit.

"We can still go somewhere else," she whispered to Matin. She barely moved her lips, but she was confident he'd hear her. That was an advantage of loving an elf man.

"We're here now."

They stepped forward, and suddenly it was their turn to have their phones scanned.

"Tamzin Herrick," Mister Hibiscus said. Today his shirt was splashed with red poppies and blades of wheat.

She nodded.

"Well, well." He coughed, and he quickly unwrapped a eucalyptus lozenge. He put it in his mouth and jerked his head towards the door. "In you go."

Tamzin froze, breathing in the smell of eucalyptus with an undertone of polish. "Do I—"

"And Matin Campania." He added something in a lower voice.

She felt Matin stiffen.

Someone cleared her throat behind them.

"We'd better move."

They shuffled forward, and Tamzin breathed in deeply again, taking in Matin's comforting scent.

"It can't be," Matin murmured.

Tamzin glanced up and saw his face, always fair-skinned,

had paled almost to skim milk. She squeezed his hand. "That's Wayne Ellington—one of the owners. What did he say to you?"

"I'll tell you later."

"Do you know him from somewhere?"

"Wait." Matin came to a stop beside another booth which had not been there at the time of their unsanctioned visit. A young woman whose badge said *Project Twenty-Five* was handing out small electronic devices.

"These are our talking guides," she said brightly, as if not repeating herself for the tenth time. "The talkers allow you to enjoy an immersive experience as you move among the installations. You can access the menu at any time and choose the level of detail you want to hear. Level One gives you a few basic facts. Level Five gives you the full program, answering questions you might ask if you visited the protagonists. However, since this is Opening Day, we ask that you keep the devices set to Level One. A touch screen in each installation will allow you to view short stereo clips. Your talker will prompt you to touch the screen when you reach the appropriate time. Touch the red menu button to pause the talker at any point.

"Since only one group may view a specific installation at a time, we have set a red-green light system. You will be prompted when it is time to move on. If you want the full immersion, you may revisit us at a later time."

Matin took one of the devices, saying nothing. Tamzin thanked the young woman, although she had little idea of how to use the thing. She was interested in finding Breezy and Clem, and she hoped some details would be forthcoming. She inserted an earpiece and switched on the device as indicated.

She'd expected the sound to be tinny, but the playback was clear.

She glanced at Matin, who, with his background in music production, must be finding this much more intuitive than she did.

He gave her a nod, and she focused on the audio.

Welcome to Project Twenty-Five, an immersive experience and, we believe, a new artform which has been twenty-five years in the making. You will hear how it came about when you reach Room Zero. For now, please enter Room Ten, which you should see in front of you, and enjoy our complimentary taster experience.

Tamzin turned and found the panel with the dog door. This now sported a large number ten instead of the pencilled card.

Step through the door, and back to December, twenty-nineteen, the audio urged.

Tamzin walked in and peered about. The room looked much as it had in torchlight, except that the lighting was rigged to suggest late afternoon.

She glanced at the dog bed. There was a stuffed bear, but at this distance, she couldn't tell if it was the one she and Matin had prepared or not.

The voice changed to an accented one she knew.

Breezy Barrett.

She was glad she had not brought Fou.

This is a utility room belonging to a house in Parson Bay, New South Wales. The house is inhabited by Clemency and Aubree Barrett, or, as they prefer to be known, Clem and Breezy. They have been a couple for many years, and they made it official in two-thousand-and-seventeen, just before they moved to Parson Bay. Clem is the homemaker, who runs a small mail-order plant business. She sings alto in the church choir. Breezy works for a temping agency. Both are keen gardeners. They also enjoy walking their dog, Fou, a rescue they gave one another as a wedding present.

Since arriving at the bay, the women have indulged their passion for all things Victorian. They belong to a group called Dames with Dogs and they enjoy many cultural pursuits.

In this room, which they refer to as Fou's Mud Room, you will see evidence of many of their interests. Fou's belongings are kept here, including his favourite stuffed toy. Garden tools line the walls, and wet-weather gear hangs waiting for rainy days. The corduroy capes you see hanging by the coats were made by Breezy according to a genuine Victorian pattern.

To see a short clip of this couple, press the red button on the windowsill. More footage is available at Level Five, when you purchase the all-day experience.

The voice ceased, and Tamzin turned to stare wonderingly at Matin. He moved over to the window, which had a painted screen showing the garden Tamzin had visited with Florida Klim.

At the touch of the button, the scene blanked out. It was replaced by an image of the inside of the room. For a moment it was still, then the dog door trembled, and opened. A stocky and familiar figure came through. Fou paused and looked over his shoulder before heading for his dog bed, where he climbed in and began to chew a disreputable bear.

The main door opened, and the two women entered in a swirl of capes.

"That bear is filthy," the taller one said.

"As long as it stays in the mud room that doesn't matter," the other responded. "Have we time for a touch-up session? My roots are showing." She bent over, presenting the top of her head to her partner.

"Tomorrow, hon. I'll get dinner started."

Tall Clem opened an interior door and stepped through.

Breezy opened the fridge and prepared a meal for Fou. As she bent to put it on the floor, the film faded.

It was quiet for a few seconds, before the lighting dimmed. The audio said pleasantly, *Breezy and Clem Barrett hope you enjoyed your visit, and that you will return for the all-day experience in which they will introduce some of their many interests. Bookings are required. For more information about this couple, scan the qrt code. Now, please step outside. It's time to visit the next installation.*

Tamzin said, "How odd. Do you think there's anything on

the website about contact details? Or in their full-day experience? Or is that just classic bait-and-switch?"

"I don't know. I don't think we can look it up here because other people are waiting."

Please step outside, the audio repeated. The room lights flashed.

Tamzin jumped. She felt unnervingly as if she were trapped in an electronic game.

Matin took her arm and they stepped back into the main gallery, crossing paths with a group of three waiting to enter.

"We'll have to keep moving, or we'll hold things up for everyone else." Matin seemed to have recovered his equilibrium. "I take it those women were the ones you know?"

"Yes. I wonder how they got to be part of this."

The audio chimed in again before Matin could answer.

You should now see Door Nine. When the previous visitors have left, step through the door, and back to September, twenty-seventeen.

A group of four strangers, looking as bemused as Tamzin felt, stepped out a few minutes later.

Tamzin and Matin entered, and Tamzin saw what she expected, the bedroom where they had sought Fou.

The lighting suggested night. Two bed lamps, one with a mismatched globe, bathed the coffee-and-cream quilt in a yellow glow.

The voice, now a man's, took on an Australian accent.

Welcome to a bedroom in a suburb of Canberra, in the Australian Capital Territory, in September twenty-seventeen. This room belongs to Tim and Amy Keats, a childless couple in their fifties. Tim works in hardware. He enjoys DIY, but his skills don't match his vision. He still has a flatpack he bought in twenty-fourteen. Amy, who works in quality control at a local supermarket, has a catalogue habit. Tim says her taste is stuck somewhere back in the nineteen-seventies. He expects momentarily to encounter a black velvet blanket with Elvis picked out in sequins . . .

The clip associated with this room showed a woman in un-flattering leggings down on her knees, apparently trying to reach something under the bed. After a bit she muttered, "Gotcha," and got to her feet. She turned, red-faced, grey hair hanging over the shoulders of an oversized and sagging shirt with a zigzag pattern. Her face contorted as she stared straight into the camera. "You beast, Tim! You might have waited until I got my face on. I thought we agreed."

"Ah-ah, we agreed to act naturally."

"Give me that!" The woman snatched at the camera, and the film tipped and blurred before it focused on a balding man bent over with his hands on his knees.

"Dammit, Amy!"

The screen blanked, then cleared, showing the same couple wearing night clothes. They climbed self-consciously into bed and lay down decorously side by side. The woman picked up a catalogue and the man started tinkering with his phone.

The film faded, with the same promise of entrance and exit interviews and more footage being available when they returned for the whole day experience.

"I wonder what *that* costs," Tamzin muttered.

"Presumably however much someone is prepared to pay for the privilege of eavesdropping on ordinary lives," Matin said.

Urged out of the bedroom, Tamzin and Matin entered Room Eight, the kitchen belonging to Bryn and Angharad Thomas in the small outback town of Jingleup, in Western Australia. The date was a winter day in twenty-fifteen.

Bryn and Angharad, according to the audio, had met at a Cymru Ball on a cruise ship in nineteen ninety-six. Their holiday romance had merged into a long-distance relationship for eighteen months before Bryn moved to Jingleup to be with Angharad. They had expanded their interest in their heritage into a homestay and hospitality business, focusing on all things Welsh.

The clip, unlike the other two, showed the couple dressed in hiking clothes, backpacking up a mountain trail, and greeting another party.

Room Seven was up on the mezzanine level. Another group was already on the staircase, so Tamzin put her hand on Matin's arm and indicated her talker before switching it to pause. "Have you seen enough?" she asked.

Matin said, "We'll have to push past a lot of people waiting to come in if we go out now."

"I suppose so." She added, "I wonder if those people are still running their business in Western Australia? It sounds a bit perilous."

"Maybe that's why they agreed to take part in this project. They must have been paid. What we saw might be only a fraction of the information gathered. There were a lot of things in the kitchen the audio didn't mention. That book, for example."

"That makes sense. I wonder if they were approached directly, or if they answered an ad."

"If you ever catch up with Breezy and Clem, you can ask them how *they* got involved."

"Very true. They'd obviously know about it. So would whoever created this show. Do you think it really took twenty-five years? Or is that part of the illusion? It would be possible to source newspapers and magazines from a few years ago. Or it could be created, the way they do for films."

Matin said, "If it was created in the past year or so, they paid a lot of attention to detail, right down to the use-by dates on the cans." He tapped her shoulder as the prompt spoke in her ear.

Proceed up the stairs to Room Seven.

"Shall we?" Matin asked.

Tamzin shrugged. "Why not?"

CHAPTER SIXTEEN: REVEALED

Tamzin Herrick, March 1st, 2020

Tamzin waited for Matin to enter Room Seven, pausing to adjust her talker. She must have failed to pause it properly, because the speech began in the middle of a sentence. She was still looking for a reverse function when she stepped through the door into a brightly lit sitting room of an open plan design with a kitchen table at one end.

She felt her eyes widen as she stared uncomprehendingly at the room. Unlike the first three, this one was bland and generic, with down-at-heel furniture. The table had a box of groceries, and a hose and brush, of the type used for cleaning cars, was propped inside the door. A book of crosswords rested on the table, and a slightly tired dried arrangement had dropped some leaves on a coffee table.

"*Bleddy hell!*" She swayed, clapping her hand over her mouth.

"Mistress?" Matin took her by the arm and led her to sit on a sagging couch, upholstered in brown vinyl.

I know this couch. There's the ragged bit where —

"Oh God. Oh, God."

Matin jerked the earpiece out of her ear and hit pause on his to silence it.

"Tamzin — you know this place?"

"Yes!" Her voice came out in a cracked squeak. "This is the house I lived in at Macquarie Bay when I was Rochelle! God, Matin — I have to get out of here!"

Matin rubbed her back. "I can see you want to — but I think we should listen to the audio. It might be just a coincidence."

She nodded numbly. "I lost my place, though."

Matin took her talker and adjusted a few buttons. "Now, it should start at the beginning."

He put his arm around her, and they listened together.

This is the family room of a rental house in Macquarie Bay, in November, twenty-twelve. For the past three years, this house has been the home of Don and Amelia Marlowe.

Tamzin heard herself give a low moan.

Don has a mobile computer repair business called Doctor Don Wholistic Health for Computers, while Amelia, or Milly as she prefers to be called, works part time at Flowers and Showers, the local florist.

The Marlowes enjoy the beachy vibe of the town. They go for long walks on the sands, and Don belongs to the sailing club. Milly likes to challenge her brain with crosswords and other literary puzzles. They miss their daughter, Rochelle, who left home some time ago. Milly hopes to hear from her soon at the old donandmilly virtual ink address.

Tamzin had difficulty catching her breath.

Matin paused the audio again before asking if she felt up to seeing the clip.

She nodded, unable to speak.

The beach view faded to show Milly and Don clearing up breakfast. Milly wore a pink overall and was clearly ready for work. They conversed amiably, debating whose turn it was to deal with dinner.

Don answered a call on his mobile. "Doctor Don — okay, what's it doing?" He put his hand over the speaker and said, "Fish and chip shop — want that for dinner, Mills?"

Milly held up her hand with her forefinger and thumb forming an affirmative circle.

The clip ended, but Tamzin stayed where she was, hunched over.

Matin said quietly, "Mistress, those were your parents?"

"Y-yes. Ada and Mister Sinister. Oh God, oh God, how did *they* get mixed up in this?"

He was silent.

She turned and said, "Don't you dare say *coincidence,* because I can't accept that. There's only so much colliding of worlds and degrees of separation I can swallow."

He nodded, and he said soberly, "I agree. If this is coincidence, it has a very long arm."

"Besides — why would they apply or even agree to do this? For God's sake, they were in hiding! Why would they want to attract attention?"

Move along, please, the audio said, out of the blue.

Tamzin considered throwing the talker against the wall as Garret Rosebay had flung his coffee cup at Wildwood Studio. Her memory of that meltdown made her hold her fire.

If you fall apart here, there might be no coming back from it.

She turned slowly to Matin. "We'd better go, but please, if I look like throwing a tantrum, or going berserk with a rolling pin, will you stop me?"

"I may well help you!" he said with the steely note she heard so seldom.

She held tightly to his hand as they left the room and moved along to Room Six. Here, they had to wait for the previous visitor to come out. She gave them a cheerful thumbs-up. "I'm so coming back for the all-day experience!"

Tamzin felt her heart beating hard.

Please let this room feature a family of six cheerful Germans.

Matin opened the door.

Oh, God.

She was ripped back in time to her bedroom as it had been in the late spring of two thousand and nine.

This is the home of Guy Herrick and his partner, Adeline Burns, who live in Sydney with their daughter, Tamzin. Guy works . . .

There was a roaring in Tamzin's ears. She stepped forward,

and she sat down on her bed, seeing the neat blue quilt. Her paintings, romantic representations of elves, were thumb-tacked on the walls, and a shelf held books on folklore and music. The program to a school musical lay on the floor. *Tintagel Unchained.*

She got up and walked across to her desk. School texts lay open as if she had been revising — which of course, she had — eleven years before.

She flipped through an atlas and came upon a program for the 2008 Turnover Exhibition. A note was scrawled across it in handwriting she remembered.

Schat- Chips at 4? D.

She moaned.

"Tamzin?" An arm came around her and she turned her face into a warm chest. For a few seconds she half-expected to feel the buttons of a school uniform shirt against her cheek.

Love you, schat . . .

Oh, Dequan — I love you too.

She inhaled, shuddering.

Green peas. This is Matin. She took a step back, and a discordant sound made her stagger. She had almost fallen over her old guitar.

She turned and picked it up, and she plucked a few strings. It was in tune, but the sound was dull and pedestrian when compared with her magical fiddle. She barely remembered how to form the chords.

"Let's get out of here," she said. She propped the guitar against the desk, then looked up at the paintings she had done when she was seventeen. She remembered being so proud of them, but they, like the guitar, seemed crudely formed when she compared them with what she could do now.

All slanting eyes and winged brows . . . bows and arrows, braids and tossing hair. What did I think I was doing — painting the cast of Tolkien Revisited?

The clip showed Adeline Burns and Guy Herrick watching

164

television in the lounge room she remembered, but she barely registered what they were watching.

She left her old bedroom without a backward glance and moved, almost calmly, onwards to Room Five, where another kitchen awaited her.

This is the home of Henry "Hank" Browning and his partner Doctor Ainsley Browning. Their daughter, Cleo, is a Scout. Doctor Browning's interest in nutrition . . .

The clip, which she viewed with a feeling of being very far away, showed Doctor Browning entering the kitchen with a paper bag from which vegetables spilled out. She began preparing them while talking over her shoulder to someone out of shot.

Presently, Hank come up and made dandelion coffee.

"Are you ready, Cleo?"

There was no answer.

"Cleo?"

Doctor Browning turned and gave Hank a meaningful look. He walked out of shot and returned, leading a sulky-looking girl by the arm. She was dressed in school uniform.

"Go and get changed, Cleo. Dinner will be ready in a minute, and your dad has to get petrol before you go to Scouts."

The girl, who was about twelve, looked mulish. She shrugged her arm away from her father and departed.

The parents exchanged another look.

The vision faded.

Tamzin cleared her throat. "I think that must have happened soon after we moved. I hadn't got used to the new diet and I hadn't made any new friends." She added, in a burst of angry humour, "God, was I really that sullen? No wonder they didn't look for Rochelle when she ran away."

She flinched as the people visiting Room Four gave her a second look. Did they really see that sulky twelve-year-old still present in her twenty-eight-year-old self?

Room Four took her back to Jade Eliot's time, to a garden

shed where mountain bikes rested on brackets. A poster of ponies hung from one wall, and some tools lay scattered on a bench. A lawnmower, still gummed up with sludgy grass that must have been cut weeks ago, stood askew in a corner.

The clip showed Mister Sinister, in his Jay Eliot shorts and cap, fixing the chain on one of the bikes. His wife Annis came in with an open bottle of beer. "I'm going to that thing at the school. Can you keep an eye on Jade?"

"Where is she?"

"Watching telly. I might be late home. Some of the mums are going on to that new café at the quay."

"Nice to be some people."

"Sure is!"

The green stone ring on Annis' hand twinkled as she pretended to preen.

Room Three was a caravan, neatly divided and flowing into an annex.

Step back with us to nineteen-ninety-eight . . . It's June, and in this Queensland caravan live Macdonald "Mac" Stevenson, his sister, Ashley, and Ashley's daughter, Abigail Angela, who is known as Abbie.

Mac makes a patchy living from freelance writing, while Ashley is a music teacher. She also works as an entertainer for children's parties. Abbie loves ballet. She hopes to be a dancer when she grows up.

The caravan is small, but well appointed. Ashley's guitar has its own bracket to free up floor space, and both beds fold into the wall. Abbie's bunk bed can be extended to make a table. Mac sometimes jokes that living with his sister and niece has dragged him out of his spiritual home in the 'sixties. Mac's fiancée, Julia, is working overseas with Medics Abroad. He writes to her often, but her return correspondence is sporadic. Some of their correspondence is available to read when you buy the All-Day Experience.

The clip showed the outside of the caravan. Mac sat in a deck chair, peering short-sightedly through his specs at a sock he was darning. Ashley, dressed in a wrap skirt with an Indian print, sat playing the guitar while a serious little girl in a tutu and ballet bun twirled and swooped. Ashley was smiling, but the child Abbie seemed uncomfortable.

She might well be. How can you dance ballet to an acoustic guitar?

"That was you." Matin's voice was soft.

"Yes—how did you know?"

"I don't think I would have if I hadn't seen your *life in pictures* folder. I'd have recognised that couple anywhere, too, from your picture. Brother and sister, though?"

"I'm sure they weren't. I can remember when I had to start calling Daddy 'Uncle Mac.' It was all part of our *let's pretend and isn't this lovely fun* game. As for a fiancée . . . I don't know if she existed or not. I don't remember ever meeting her . . . only—"

"What, my dolphin?"

"I just remembered Uncle Mac went away for a few days with Shades. That was just before we left the caravan. Mummy took Abbie—me—to a city, maybe Melbourne, to see a ballet. We dressed up in new clothes. When we came back it was to the house in Adelaide. Uncle Mac never came, but Dad did."

"I wondered when *he* was going to come into the story," Matin said.

"Shades. He came to see us every so often, but it wasn't until I was Cleo that I started associating him with our all-change moves. He used to call me by the wrong name. I think he was at the ballet. I remember Mummy talking to a man while we were waiting to go in."

Someone rapped on the door.

The lights in the caravan flashed repeatedly.

"Time's up," Matin said. He thumbed *pause* and held the earpiece between them so Tamzin could hear the increasingly impatient instructions for them to move on.

"Are you ready for Room Two?" he asked gently.

She nodded. "We'll be visiting Angie's house next. I don't know where it was."

She was fatalistically prepared for what was to come, so it was hardly a shock to enter a child's bedroom, lined with dolls, picture books and bins of building blocks.

A pink bed stood under the window, and the curtains featured butterfly princesses.

This is where Angela "Angie" Blake lives with her parents, Chad and Alison. The place is Delmsford in Tasmania, and the year is nineteen ninety-six.

The clip showed the delivery of the princess bed, a flatpack. Chad and Alison put it together with minimal fuss. The clip faded out and resumed to show Angie, wearing a big *I'm Five* badge on her pink butterfly princess T-shirt, walking into the room holding her parents' hands. She had on a blindfold which was whisked off . . .

Surprise!

The amazed joy in her younger self's face dazzled Tamzin for a second before she recalled the aftermath.

"Angie had that bed for just a few weeks before we moved. They said the bed wouldn't fit in the caravan." She lifted her face to Matin. "Were they being gratuitously cruel?"

"I don't know. It depends on how much in control they were of their moves and the characters they inhabited."

"It does . . . but I think they were very much in control. They weren't acting. They *were* those people. Remember Tim Keats? *He* had a flatpack he'd had since twenty-fourteen . . . when he didn't exist. At least I don't think he did. I've lost track of the dates a bit. And there he is as Chad Blake, putting one together in a few minutes."

"You did say they were chameleons." He tucked her face into his shoulder, shutting out the sight of the princess bed. "You didn't recognise Tim Keats as your father?"

"No. He looked so different, and I had no reason to think I

knew him. It's so long since I saw them. And we never got a good look at Bryn and Angharad — they were out hiking with woolly hats pulled over their hair."

She felt Matin kiss the top of her head. "You do realise what this means."

"Oh, yes. Clem and Breezy. I've been lodging my *own parents'* dog. Clem though — no wonder she stayed in the background and never said much. Singing alto! Why didn't I see it?"

"Chameleons," he said.

"And those capes — their Victoriana. Those hid their outlines, and we all tend to focus on the unusual. Masquerading isn't about false beards and fake scars. It's about *living* in the character."

The lights flashed and the audio became insistent. Tamzin stood back. She removed her earpiece and dropped it on the floor. She lifted her spy-heeled shoe.

"*No*, mistress." Matin pulled her away.

"I want to!"

"No tantrums."

"You said you'd *help* me!"

"I will — but later." He picked up the earpiece and held it in his palm. "Are you going to put this in, or should I keep it safe?"

"I'll behave."

She put it in her ear.

Proceed to Room One.

Tamzin growled.

Below her rage and her confusion lurked a trembling fear. She had been waiting for so long, and now it seemed likely she would come face to face with a past she remembered only in fragmented flashbacks.

CHAPTER SEVENTEEN: ROOM ONE

Tamzin Herrick, March 1st, 2020

Matin waited for Tamzin to open the door to Room One. His steady presence at her back made it possible to touch the entry button.

She stepped inside a three-sided porch. The open end was painted with an impressive *trompe-l'œil* . . . at least, that was what she thought it was, until she realised it was moving. The sound of waves swished in her ears, and she looked out over a shingle beach with a long wave flowing in to tinkle the pebbles.

She sat down on a rattan settee, staring about with glazing eyes.

Matin sat beside her.

"You know where we are," she said.

"Yes, mistress. This is Fiddle Bay."

She glanced about the porch. "I don't know this house, but it can't be far from Fiddler's Rest. Oh, *God,* no wonder I was drawn to the place."

A child's ride-on toy stood next to the couch, and a beach towel printed with palm trees was tossed over the rail. A potted peace lily rested on a glass-topped outdoor table, along with two floral mugs and a harmonica. A collar and leash had been coiled on the table, embracing the potted lily. Tamzin leaned over to read the tag. *Barney.* It was followed by a telephone number she didn't know.

"Do you remember this?" Matin asked.

"Not at all. I just know the place because I recognise the bay." She indicated the scene in front of her. She half expected to smell the salt, and to feel the sea breeze on her face.

She pressed the audio button and held tightly to Matin's hand.

A voice she remembered and disliked began to speak.

This is the porch of Number Fifteen, Beach Parade, Fiddle Bay. The date is sometime in October, nineteen-ninety-four. For five years, this has been the home of Paul and Adelie. Their daughter Alexandra was a surprise package, but in her way, she was instrumental in the step Paul and Adelie are about to take. The contents of the porch are exactly as the family left them when they drove down to Station Pier yesterday.

The voice ended, and Tamzin unhesitatingly accessed the clip.

It was disappointingly brief.

It showed two young people seated on the rattan couch. The woman, dressed in a suit that suggested office work, had her blonde hair dressed in a French pleat. The young man, lounging beside her, held a sleeping child. He turned to the woman and said, "Ready, Peng?"

She nodded.

Okay. We're probably not your average family. Paul's lot are posh. Mine aren't. The only thing they have in common is a desire to drag us back into the fold.

Separate folds, the man put in.

Yes. We thought we'd got away, but then, when Alexandra was born, we needed some help. I was catching up on the schooling I missed, and Paul is – was – often away on the road, so we accessed his trust fund – yes, he has one, the wanker – and hired a nanny to look after Alexandra.

Lucida was recommended by a friend.

Some friend! the man said.

Think Nanny dearest. *Think* Single White Female. *Think* bunny boiler.

Think Mary Poppins. *Then think bloody* Nanny Lu.

We're going away. We won't be able to get any more trust fund money, and so we're doing something we always wanted . . . we're going to change our names and live as other people.

The scene ended and Tamzin sat in shock.

"Lucida. Nanny Lu."

Someone tapped on the door. The lights flashed.

Matin helped her up. "Now you know."

"I don't! They didn't give surnames . . . that was like a rehearsed presentation."

"We'd better move," he said as the lights flashed again.

Someone banged on the door.

"Why don't they just come in?"

"I don't think the door will open until we go out." He paused and added, "Are you ready for Room Zero?"

"Yes. If there's anything to find out, it will be there."

CHAPTER EIGHTEEN: ROOM ZERO

Tamzin Herrick, March 1st, 2020

Room Zero proved different from the others.
To gain entry, they had to scan their tickets again.

Inside, instead of a mock-up of a room, they found a gallery lined with curtained alcoves, like change rooms or photo booths.

Another gallery employee awaited them. "Hello, Tamzin and Matin. I hope you've found the experience so far interesting?"

"Interesting!" Tamzin heard her voice crack.

The woman looked at her sharply. "Is anything wrong?"

"Why should anything be wrong?"

"I don't know. Why should it?"

Matin said quietly, "Have you seen the installations?"

"Yes—well, not since they were animated. Why? Did something not work?"

Matin said, "It's hard to say, since the intention isn't too plain."

She crinkled her brow. "It's snapshots into random lives, taken through twenty-five years. It's a clever concept, and the rooms are absolutely authentic. Each room was measured, scanned and photographed in detail so the installation rooms could exactly replicate the originals. The items and furnishings are the real things, with the exception of flooring."

"What's this then?" Tamzin asked, indicating the booths.

"This is an optional addendum for the experience. It's

basically the creators talking about their experiences while dealing with this undertaking."

"They're here?"

"No, it's an unedited talking heads production. You may find it informative, but you might also prefer to leave the illusion intact. It's up to you."

"We'll go in," Tamzin said.

"Fine. I think the people in booth nine are about finished — yes, there's the green light."

The door to one of the booths opened and a middle-aged couple dressed in Lycra and dangling bike helmets came out, blinking and laughing.

"What a ride," the man said. "How do you top that, Penguin?"

The woman hit him with her helmet.

"You can go on in now," the gallery employee said, indicating booth nine.

"No . . . I've changed my mind," Tamzin said.

Matin looked down at her in consternation.

She handed her device to the woman, turned on her heel and headed for the door, pulling Matin with her.

When they were on the spiral stair, she whispered, "Those two bikers — we've got to catch them."

Matin responded by increasing their speed down the steps.

They followed the bikers, keeping them in sight, until they stepped out into the balmy Adelaide evening.

Mister Hibiscus was still processing tickets as they passed.

The couple strolled up to where familiar bicycles were padlocked to a railing. They hesitated, then the man said, "Coffee first?"

"Sure —"

They turned and headed into the coffee shop that served the gallery patrons.

Matin paused. "Better let them order . . . I'll be back in a minute."

"Where—" Tamzin was left open-mouthed as he darted back the way they had come.

She turned to look at the door to the coffee shop. *Galleria Coffee.*

What if they get takeaways?

She steadied herself. They were travelling by bicycle. That hardly suggested takeaway coffee. It was difficult enough to carry it while walking.

She waited.

Matin came back, looking white and strained. "I'm sorry about that. I just needed a word."

"With Mister Hibiscus?"

"With Wayne Ellington. Great bogle, it's as plain as the nose on my face!"

Tamzin turned wondering eyes to him.

"Remember a famous person called Ellington?"

"Um—oh, you mean Duke Ellington? The jazz player?"

"Duke," he said heavily. "That was what Aunt Mim called *him.* Your man Shades."

"*Shades?*"

"In the flesh. He didn't bother to deny it." He smiled bitterly. "I didn't even need a compulsion. He just said, 'Still playing catch-up with the cruel, cruel world, Matty-the-elf-boy? How's your auntie?'"

"The creep! Did you hit him?"

Matin showed his teeth. "No. I did something much worse."

"I'm *so* glad. You can tell me what it was later—but now we'd better get into the shop and sort out my precious parents."

Hand in hand, they stepped forth to a confrontation that had been almost ten years in the making.

The story concludes in *Being Tamzin 7*

ABOUT THE AUTHOR

Lark Westerly loves weaving stories about characters who grow and change while remaining true to themselves. The *Being Tamzin* series has seven books, and the mysteries the characters need to solve were also mysteries for Lark to unpick. Sometimes, that meant moving back to an earlier book to plant a clue. At other times, the clue was there already, put in unintentionally. *So that's how it happened! Ah, so* this *is why he said that back then.* Now *I see!* The revelations were great fun for Lark, and she hopes they delight her readers just as much.

The developments in *Being Tamzin 6* were particularly complicated to plan as everything draws together in preparation for the finale.

Lark lives on the island of Tasmania, where she is never bored. She has a husband, two adult children, two grandchildren and some dogs. She enjoys walking, reading, photography, generally creating microcosms and researching for whatever she's writing. For *Being Tamzin 6,* this involved mostly a close rereading of earlier books in the series and much to-ing and fro-ing to match up dates and places.

Daylight and Garret's story had to resolve, and Emily had to appear in the flesh. The big revelation about Tamzin's parents had to unfold, triggered by the unlikely catalyst of Fou.

The series will conclude in *Being Tamzin 7,* where the final revelations come. There is still one more blast from the past, and we also return to Nelis Winter and Xavier Partridge for the first time since *Being Tamzin 1.*

For more about Lark and her stories, check out her

homepage at https://larksinger.weebly.com

The Being Tamzin companion page, with annotated character lists, terms and places *and* a big spoiler page, is at https://beingtamzin.weebly.com

www.ingramcontent.com/pod-product-compliance
Lightning Source LLC
Chambersburg PA
CBHW060817120626
46557CB00001B/248